JENIKA SNOW

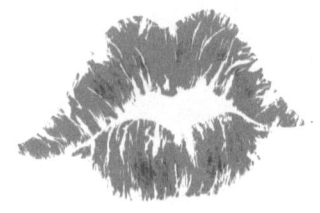

EVERNIGHT PUBLISHING ®

www.evernightpublishing.com

Copyright© 2016

Jenika Snow

Editor: Karyn White

Cover Artist: Sour Cherry Designs

Jacket Design: Jay Aheer

ISBN: 978-1-77339-005-5

JENIKA SNOW

DEDICATION

This is dedicated to all the readers, and the Crescent Snow Street Team. Thank you all for your support, kind words, and for wanting to read my crazy stories.

JENIKA SNOW

LUCIEN'S WAR

The Brothers of Menace, 3

Jenika Snow

Copyright © 2014

Chapter One

Lucien stood against the garage wall, the cigarette he shouldn't be smoking hanging from between his lips, and staring at the man currently strung up like a tied hog. The man Cain had brought to the clubhouse was the same one that had nearly raped Cain's now-adult daughter years ago. Cain had been in prison for the last nine years, locked up for killing this exact bastard. Someone had called the cops before he could finish the guy off, and the other MC member had held the rage inside, just waiting until he was released so he could finish the job. Lucien couldn't even imagine being a father and having some fucker force himself on his little girl. It didn't matter that Fallina was twenty-five now, or that she was doing well in her life and teaching. She had still had to go through that, and Cain hadn't gotten the vengeance he desperately needed.

Well, he was getting it now.

Cain had done the beating, and although they had been in this garage behind the clubhouse for the last few hours, Cain was unstoppable. The fucker, who looked nearly dead as it was, had his arms above his head, a piece of rope secured around his wrists, and was hanging suspended from one of the beams. He was passed out at the moment but Cain walked over to grab a bucket of ice water Kink had brought him, and threw it on the man. The would-be rapist sputtered and came back to consciousness. Cain took a step back, took off the once white tee he wore, which was now stained red from blood, and tossed it aside. Lucien inhaled from his cigarette and blew the smoke out softly until a cloud covered his vision. It dispersed, and he watched as Cain grabbed a pair of brass knuckles from the workbench, slipped them on, and moved back to the guy.

"Please, stop. I was drunk," the man sputtered out. Blood dripped out of his nose and mouth, and fell onto his chest and the ground.

Cain swung out without answering, and connected the brass knuckles with the man's face. He howled out in pain, struggled on his bonds, but then started to slowly still. Blood was a continuous flow from him, and a small pool was now on the floor beneath him.

"My daughter kept saying stop, didn't she? And if I hadn't come when I did you would have damaged her even more than you already did." Cain said in a deadly calm voice. "But you didn't stop for Vi—" Cain stopped talking right away. He shook his head, inhaled deeply for a moment, and Lucien wondered what he had been about to say. The rage on Cain's face over this situation was the fiercest Lucien had ever seen on a brother. Malice moved up beside Cain, handed him the bottle of whiskey, and then moved back toward Kink, who was leaning against the other side of the building.

"The guy's about to take a dive, brother," Lucien said, took one more inhale from his cigarette, and then dropped it on the floor to snub it out. "If you don't finish him off he'll die from blood loss or shock, and you'll miss giving him that final blow."

Cain nodded, took another drink from the bottle of liquor while he stared at the man he was about to end, and then set the bottle on the floor. "You're right. I better end this now before this fucker passes out again and can't feel how I make the last seconds of his life even more painful." He went over to the workbench again, grabbed a nine-inch serrated hunting knife, and walked over to the man, who was struggling to breathe now. Most likely blood was starting to pool in his lungs, so Cain needed to be quick before the motherfucker suffocated in his own fluids. Cain grabbed the guy's chin, turned his swollen and beaten face up so he was forced to look at Cain, and bared his teeth.

"If you would have died nine years ago when I had you, your death would have been far quicker. But for the last nine years while I was locked away all I could picture was all the ways I was going to take your life." Cain took the blade and ran it along each side of the asshole's face. The skin opened up instantly, but there wasn't much sound that came from the man.

He would be dead soon either at Cain's hands, or because his body had had enough.

"You made my daughter afraid for a long fucking time, and although she is strong and living her life now, your fucking existence still haunts her." Cain stabbed the man in the gut. "Your death won't make her feel any better, because she won't know what happened. I can't tell her what I did, but she will know that her fear doesn't need to control her anymore." Cain moved the blade up, opening up the prick's stomach like a hot knife going through butter. "I could have let you live your life with the shame of what you did to my daughter, and probably other young girls, but killing you will sate this sadistic monster inside of me that has been itching to take you out." He continued to move the blade up slowly, and the man gurgled, struggled fruitlessly, and when Cain twisted the blade the life faded from the rapist's eyes.

The silence that filed the room was deafening, but there was also this release that seemed to come from Cain like the relief that covered his face. He took a step back, and the knife he held dripped the red, viscous fluid onto the ground. Cain stared at each of them, set the knife down, and picked up the bottle. He drank the alcohol until nothing was left.

"What the fuck am I supposed to do with the body?" Cain asked without emotion.

"We have twenty acres on this property. I'm sure we can find some place for him," Malice said in a deep voice.

"And no one will come looking for him?" Kink asked. He moved toward the guy and stared at his lifeless body.

"No, this piece of shit was living in a crack-house about two hours from here, high with a needle still in his fucking arm, and a whore draped over him sucking his dick," Cain said and took the offered cigarette Kink handed him. "Besides, I did my research on him while inside—I had some connections while locked away—and knew that once I was out I'd have everything I needed to hunt him down and finish what I started nine years ago." Cain lit the end, inhaled from the cigarette, and then exhaled. He looked down at the smoke. "You should quit this shit. It'll kill you," Cain said, took one more hit from the smoke, and then snubbed the butt out on the bottom of his shoe. "Well, if you boys are ready to get this fucking piece of dirt in the ground, I'm ready to put this shit behind me."

Lucien walked over to the corpse, unhooked him from the chain that he was attached to, and let his body fall to the floor. Kink and Malice picked him off the floor, and the four of them walked out of the garage through the backdoor, and made their way through the woods that lined the clubhouse. Lucien had grabbed a few shovels on his way out, and Kink had grabbed a flashlight. The body was draped over Malice's shoulder, and the outline of Cain leading the way was illuminated by the moonlight moving through the trees.

Over the years with the club Lucien had done some fucked up things, but they had been part of the MC, keeping everyone whole, and making sure payback was dealt. The illegal things they had done had been necessary, and he didn't regret any of it, not even what they were doing right now.

Twenty minutes later and they had dug a hole big enough to keep the body buried, and covered the asshole molester with dirt. They stood there when the hole was filled.

"You guys know you're my family," Cain said, but still had his focus on the freshly filled grave. "I have been waiting for this day since I pulled the motherfucker off my daughter all those years ago."

Lucien clapped Cain on the back. "I know, brother, and you're our family, too."

"For life," Kink said out loud.

"And we'd do anything to help you find peace and vengeance, brother," Malice stated, and moved closer to place his hand on Cain's shoulder.

Cain nodded.

"Anyone fucks with a member's kid, in any damn way, and we band together and take them out," Kink said in a deep rumble that held menace and threat.

Lucien glanced at Kink after he spoke. Although Lucien wanted Kink's eighteen-year-old daughter in the worst kind of way, he also knew he was too damn old for her, and that doing anything with her was a big fucking backstabbing idea for him to do to another brother. But when Lucien had brought Callie back to his place the night she had called him shitfaced, something in him had shifted. He had never seen her as anything more than a young woman to protect because she was family. He hadn't touched her, hadn't done anything other than think about the totally wrong fucking things that would get him shot by Kink. The man was his VP, a man he considered a brother, and a person he would lay down his life for. Trying anything with Callie, even if she was of legal age, would be a traitorous move on Lucien's part.

But Lucien still wanted Callie, and no matter how hard he stayed away, tried not to think about her, and told himself that being with her would be a betrayal, Lucien wanted her so fucking badly. He could taste it, feel it in his blood with every beat of his heart, and had this ache in his cock and balls that screamed to be inside of Callie and ease his need for her.

"Let's get drunk," Lucien said, glanced at the three men again, and then headed back to the clubhouse.

He needed to get good and trashed, because his thoughts were too fucking dangerous.

****

Callie stared around at the empty bedroom that she had stayed in most of the time when she had lived with her mother. The funeral for her mother and Dale had been uneventful, but it wasn't because the only people that had shown up were the guys from the club and a couple old ladies. The thing was, her mother had burned a lot of bridges throughout her life, using her hate, selfishness, and anger to keep her alienated from her own family. Even death couldn't have brought her mother's parents to the funeral of their only child. And that was one of the saddest things Callie had ever experienced.

Although she had gotten most of her things out of the house she had shared with her mom and her mother's boyfriend, Dale, she still found herself coming back here more times than she should. First it had been just driving past the house, but then the last two occasions she had actually come inside, walked through the rooms, and thought about all of the times her mother hadn't been there for her. Sarah had been her mom, but even thought she was dead and Callie shouldn't think such thoughts, she admitted to herself only that she hadn't been a very good mother. She had neglected Callie, ignored her, yelled at her, scolded her, and told her on more than one occasion that she should have been aborted because then Kink wouldn't have been in her life. What mother said those things—did those things—to her own child?

Callie felt her tears start to fill her eyes, and hated that fact. She didn't want to cry over the past, didn't want to feel any kind of anger toward her mother anymore because she was dead, and what was the point? She pushed away the stray tears that had fallen, and moved away from her bedroom and back down the stairs. She had a lot to do, a lot of things to keep her mind off of what had happened. She needed to think about college, finish filling out applications, and then leave everything behind. Her dad and Cookie had been great, and she had never thought she'd feel any kind of close connection with her father's old lady. Maybe it was because Cookie was a tortured soul, and had still prevailed despite everything against her?

Callie had been staying with her dad and Cookie at his house, and although she liked having them around, liked the fact her father had always been there for her, had tried to always do right by her, and had never let his violent and dangerous MC life seep into her and tarnish anything about her, being in River Run was really hard. She thought back to the night she had been wasted at a college party with her shitty then-boyfriend. That night could have been really bad, and gone down a totally different way, but then she had called Lucien Silver, The Brothers of Menace President. Just thinking about him had this chill of awareness moving through her. At forty years old, he was over twice her age, deadly and lethal, and not because he had the title of being the leader of an outlaw motorcycle club. He just carried this air of being able to kill a man with his bare hands, that he wasn't to be messed with, and he was so wrong for her on every damn level.

Callie was an eighteen-year-old virgin who had partied hard during high school, had had a douchebag boyfriend, and now wanted Lucien like she wanted to breathe. What did she really know about anything out in life? Also, her father was the VP of Lucien's club, and being with a member was a big no-no. Lucien would never be with her in any way imaginable, even if she knew he felt the same intense chemistry. Being with her would be a betrayal to Kink in Lucien's eyes, and how could she do that to either of them?

She exhaled, feeling so confused and out of place, and not knowing what her future held. What she did know was she needed to leave River Run and Lucien, because with each passing day it grew harder and harder to keep her emotions in check. Even when she had seen him at the funeral, and grief had been strong inside of her, she had thought of running up to him and just letting him hold her. God, she had wanted him to hold her so badly. But after that she hadn't seen Lucien, even when she had visited the club. It was like he was keeping away from her, and maybe that was for the best.

So going to college, staying on campus, and putting all of this behind her was the right move. At least she hoped it was, because she just wanted to tell him again that she didn't want to leave, that she didn't care if people talked, that their age difference wasn't going have anything lasting between them. She also wanted to tell him that things would work out, that what she felt wasn't just some crush an eighteen-year-old girl had on an older man. He consumed her thoughts, made her feel safe when she was with him, and she wanted so much more with him.

But maybe she *was* some stupid little girl who was fantasizing about something that would never happen? That's why she needed to leave, for her own sake so she didn't make an ass out of herself, and so she didn't tear apart a relationship between two men who considered themselves brothers.

Chapter Two

Three months later

Lucien was a sick bastard, a dirty old man, and a fucking traitor if he was being honest with himself. He thought about her, Callie Roberts, a woman he had no right even consider being with in any fashion. But he couldn't help himself. She was like the drug of choice to an addict, *his* drug of choice. She was the one woman who seemed to consume his very thoughts since he had taken her back to his house months ago. She had been drunk, nearly attacked by two thug motherfuckers, and he had talked to her when he had been laid up in bed and shot the fuck up.

He tossed back another drink, glanced at the bottle of whiskey in front of him, and saw it fade out for a second. He was drunk, wasted, totally fucking trashed, but since he had gotten shot that had been the norm. Lucien had felt himself slip further and further into a dark abyss, and no matter how many runs he went on, trying to clear his head, nothing ever helped. But it wasn't just because of the shit that had happened with the cult assholes, or the fact he had nearly died. Hell, it didn't even have to do with the crazy fucking torture they had done to the man that had fucked with Cain's daughter.

No, his darkness was coming from the fact he wanted Kink's eighteen-year-old daughter. But he knew she would be leaving for college soon, and that was a good thing, because if she had stayed in River Run he didn't know if he could control himself around her for very much longer. As it was he had been doing a pretty good job. Whenever he had seen Callie coming into the clubhouse with Cookie or Kink he had made himself scarce, because it was damn hard for him not to look at her. He tried not to stare at the woman she had become, and picture her under him as he worshipped every part of her body with his hands and tongue.

Yeah, he was a sick fucking bastard to want a woman so young, and the daughter of the man he considered a brother. It was wrong to think of her in his bed, under him, and being only *his*. Shit, she was over two decades younger than he was, a full twenty-two years his junior. She was of legal age, but he was old enough to be her father. Even thinking that, knowing that if Kink knew the fucking intimate and dirty thoughts he had for Callie he'd kill him, that didn't, *couldn't* stop Lucien from wanting her like a man tweaking for his next fix. He hadn't even touched her in a sexual way, hadn't kissed her for that matter either, but he craved her like he was addicted to her.

Kink was at the bar with Cookie, but since his old lady only worked in the kitchen now, per her request because she liked preparing the meals, Lucien didn't see her out on the main floor that often. But he knew Kink liked that she was behind the scenes. Even if Cookie was tough in her own right, and she was protected within the club walls, that didn't mean Kink liked having her around all the booze, drugs, and sex that made a common sight. Lucien couldn't blame the brother though, because if he had an old lady himself he wouldn't want her around all of this shit. The club life was rowdy, sometimes vile, and an old lady didn't need to see the shit the single club members did behind these walls.

He took another shot and felt the lingering pain in his thigh start to grow numb. Since the cult members had shot him all those months ago in the abandoned warehouse, his recovery had been slow going. Although Lucien was a stubborn asshole, refusing to do the physical therapy that Molly suggested he take part in, he was getting back to his old self. He worked out with the other members, taking it easy, but still working out with them. There were times when he was having a difficult time with the stiffness in his leg, but it was also only three months out from nearly dying.

Lucien watched as Kink took Cookie around the waist and pulled her close. He kissed her like no one was watching, that or he didn't give a shit who saw him mouth-fuck his woman. What was sad was the fact Lucien hadn't even been able to get it up since he had taken Callie back to his place. He'd tried with a couple of club pussies, even tried to tag team two of them with Ruin, but he hadn't been able to get his dick hard. Fuck, he was sexually frustrated, needed to get laid, and was pissed because he knew the only woman that would be able to help him in that department was one he could never have.

"You want a hit, prez?" Rook asked and handed Lucien the joint.

Lucien shook his head and stood. "Nah, I think I'm going to go work out, because as it is this alcohol isn't helping my nerves, and I'm not in the mood to fuck." Well, he *was* in the mood to fuck, if he could be able to be with the woman he wanted. *Callie will never be in your reach.* Lucien took another swig from the bottle, not about to tell anyone the reason he couldn't get his dick hard.

He moved past the guys playing pool, walked around the club girls dancing in front of some of the prospects, and walked past Kink and Cookie.

"Lucien," Kink called out.

He tensed, but turned around. For the last several months he had steered clear of Callie, not because he wanted to, but because it was the smart thing to do. When he had seen her at her mother's funeral, he'd had to stop himself from going to her and holding her the whole time she cried. He had talked to her, although briefly, but touching her opened up something inside of him. It made him want to tell her he'd make sure everything was okay, that he would never let anyone hurt her, because she was his, and always would be. But she wasn't his, and never would be. He couldn't betray Kink, couldn't go against club rules that said a brother was never to fuck with another member's family in any sexual way, even if that family member wanted them. Daughters were off limits, yet Lucien wanted Kink's eighteen-year-old one with a fierceness that was so damn intense he felt like he was going to go off the hinge. But even wanting Callie was betraying Kink, even if the brother had no clue the thoughts Lucien really had.

"You feeling okay?" Kink said.

"I'm good. Just got a lot on my mind these days."

Kink nodded, still with his arm around Cookie, but had this concerned look on his face. "Yeah, I know the feeling. Callie will be heading off to college for the weekend. Some kind of orientation thing or some shit, and man, I tell you, I'm already freaking out." Kink rubbed the back of his neck, and Cookie smiled.

Lucien felt this tightness in his gut, had this itchiness under his skin, and knew that he shouldn't be feeling this way over Callie leaving. This was good for her, and the fact he had kept his distance, and that she was moving away from all of this were good things. He stared at the man he considered a brother, his VP, and the father of the woman he knew he cared about more than any other female in the entire fucking planet. He was toeing the line on this, and if he did what he really wanted to do, then he'd be crossing it, hurting Kink, and possibly bringing his club down from the ramifications of it all. To tell his VP what had happened all those months ago now seemed pointless, but as he stared at the other man, he opened his mouth, about to tell Kink everything. There should be no secrets between them, yet he had kept something like this from her father, all because of what? Because he was hard up for her? Because she had asked him not to? No, it was because he loved Callie, and cared about Kink, and saying anything would be disastrous.

Yeah, he loved her, fucking loved her more than he had a right to. He had never cared about a woman for more than a few hours at a time, screwing them to show his affection, and then walking away. He could be a cold, cruel bastard, but with Callie he wanted to show her that he could be gentle, that he wasn't made up of all violence. That was what she deserved.

"Kink, man," Lucien said and swallowed past the lump in his throat. He couldn't keep this a secret anymore, because already so much time had passed.

"Hey," Pierce shouted out, his drunken ass weaving toward them, beer bottle held high. "We need to get this fucking party started, get some pussy up in here for some action, and get my horny ass fixed up." Pierce pushed between Kink and Lucien, set his beer bottle on the counter, and gestured for another from the prospect behind the counter.

"And that's our cue to get the fuck out of here," Kink said and took Cookie away from the bar. He clapped Lucien on the shoulder as he passed, but instead of Lucien speaking up he leaned on the bar and sighed.

God, what a fucking pussy he was.

Lucien stared at the front door and watched as Kink and his old lady left. He was fucked up, and needed to get out of here and clear his head. Turning away from the bar he saw Pepper, one of the club girls, moving toward him, this smile on her face, and her tits barely restrained under her top. Having no sex for this long was hard as fuck, but he was not about to go there with club pussy, or any other woman for that matter. He needed to figure out what the fuck he was going to do, and how he was going to get Callie off the brain.

"Hey there," Pepper said with this seductive grin on her face, and her hands already moving toward his chest. He took hold of her wrists and pushed her away.

"No, Pepper." Lucien turned and grabbed the shot the prospect gave him. After downing it, he knew he needed to get the fuck out of here.

"Come on, Lucien. It's been a long damn time since you were with me," Pepper said on a pout. "I want to feel that big ol' dick filling me up, baby." She grinned, her eyes slightly bloodshot, and the scent of stale cigarettes covered her. "You got someone else?"

Yes.

"I have whiskey dick, so it ain't happening tonight." Of course that was a lie, because he could have gotten hard for Callie in a fucking second, rock hard like steel just by thinking about her. And damn, he was getting a stiffie right now just as the thought of Callie slammed into his head.

"Really? Because, baby, you look like you're ready to go." Pepper grabbed his crotch, and he moved away.

That wasn't for her, for damn sure. Shaking his head at Pepper, he turned before she started grinding herself on him and headed out of the clubhouse. He'd go to his place, work out until he couldn't see straight, shower, and then rub one off while thinking about the woman that made him feel so damn on edge, and so possessive at just the thought of her. He hoped in the morning things would look a little clearer, but he wasn't holding his breath.

Chapter Three

The clubhouse was quiet, but Callie was thankful for that. It was pretty early in the morning, and although she figured either the guys at the clubhouse would be asleep or, she hoped, not there, she wasn't holding her breath. Most likely she'd see some naked club pussy lying around, beer bottles lining on the ground, and smell the stench of spilled booze and pot filling the air.

She had seen Lucien's Harley parked outside, but she hadn't noticed any other bikes or even vehicles on club property. She had gotten off lucky if Lucien was, in fact, here and alone, but the more realistic scenario was that there would be a club whore draped over him like a blanket.

Callie hadn't been thinking straight when she got in her car, the back packed with an overnight bag for her weekend trip to Baker, and then headed on the road. College was the last thing on her mind, even three months later, because she still thought about her mom, and still wanted Lucien. These last few months had made her realize he was most definitely either avoiding her, or she had been totally off base in thinking he reciprocated her feelings.

God, Callie actually loved him. Even after that one time where she stayed at Lucien's house because she had been too drunk to go home, and hadn't known whom else to go to, Lucien had only been innocent and protective in his actions toward her. He had made sure she was safe, had protected her when some thugs had tried to take advantage of her in her inebriated state, and although he was so much older than she was and was her father's club president, she still wanted him. He was all she thought about, all she craved. Not even spending time with her friend Ian could help distract her from what she wanted, and that was a too-old-for-her biker club president.

After saying goodbye for the weekend to Cookie and her dad, Callie had intended just to go right to the university, but then she had found herself pulling into the driveway of The Brothers of Menace clubhouse. She shouldn't have come here, but she had to say goodbye to Lucien, because after this weekend she'd come home, pack up her shit, and then head off to college for good. She'd put this town and him behind her, and try to start her life.

Moving through the clubhouse proved that it was empty, but that didn't stop her from continuing toward the meeting room, or wondering where everyone was. She was just thankful she wouldn't have to answer any questions as to why she had come here, or risk one of the members telling her dad that she had come to talk to Lucien. But the truth was she hadn't even thought about any of that as she drove here. No one knew what had happened to her and Lucien, how he had saved her and let her crash at his place. Although they hadn't done anything, he hadn't told Kink, as per her request. Although she had told Lucien she'd tell her dad, she hadn't yet. She was afraid of her father's anger toward a situation that hadn't been anything but innocent, of what it would do to his relationship with Lucien, and the fact he would jump to conclusions. Maybe because the clubhouse was empty aside from Lucien was fate trying to help her out?

Wishful thinking on her part.

She went into the meeting room, but it was empty. The sound of something in the back hallway had her turning and moving toward that direction. She made her way forward as if her mind and body were disconnected, and her need to do this drove her forward. She meant to just tell him goodbye, but maybe her *need* to see him, and the fact she was actually telling him she was leaving, would have him finally opening up to her? Whether he told her that he didn't want her, or finally admitted that he wanted her, too, she needed to hear him say *something*. Callie needed him to tell her *anything*. She had this feeling in the pit f her stomach every time she thought about him, every time she saw him. It grew with each passing day, consumed her, and it was close to bursting from her and taking her down.

Making her way forward, she followed the light noise that could be heard behind one of the doors at the end of the hallway. It was slightly ajar, and when she pushed it open a little more it was to see Lucien's powerful and tattooed muscular back. He was sitting at a small desk, and although she couldn't see what he was doing, she heard the sound of *clicking* and *thunking* metal against the table. She knew the sounds well, had heard them in her dad's house when he was cleaning his guns. Lucien was shirtless, and the jeans he wore were low on his narrow hips. God, she could remember what the front of him looked like all those months ago when she had been at his house and he stepped out of his bedroom. He had just gotten out of the shower, his massively muscular body toned and covered in tattoos. And then there had been the Brothers of Menace patch tattoo in the center of his chest, so big, so powerful, and screaming that he was dangerous.

Swallowing past the nervousness, she knocked on his door. He turned just his head and looked over his shoulder at her, and although she knew she was probably the last person he expected to see, he showed no emotion.

"Callie?" He said her name in that deep voice of his, the one that she had imagined many times over when she closed her eyes. He stood and turned, and she let her gaze travel over his chest. The Brothers of Menace patch tattoo took up the center of his chest, and she felt herself grow warm at the sight of his muscular and powerful form standing in front of her. He was so big compared to her, and although she had never considered herself a tiny thing, compared to him she felt just like that. They stared at each other, and after an awkward few seconds he finally spoke again.

"What are you doing here?"

"I…" She licked her lips, glanced around his room, and then focused on him again. "I just wanted to say goodbye."

He nodded slowly and then rubbed his palms on his thighs. She looked at his chest again, felt her heart flutter, and then felt her throat tighten at the thought of all the things she wanted to say.

"I'm leaving for the weekend to check out Baker and get my dorm and schedule information." She heard the tremor in her voice, knew that she was probably shaking slightly, because right now she felt like she might pass out.

He nodded. "College is good for you, Callie. You'll meet new people, learn stuff that will help you out in life, and maybe find a guy your own age that will treat you like the princess you are."

His words struck right in her heart, and she breathed out. Had he realized what he had just said? The expression on his face told her he hadn't meant to say anything like that, but the words were already out there, hanging between them, and making her long for his touch.

"Shit, I hadn't meant to say some of that." He lifted a hand and rubbed the back of his neck. The way his bicep clenched and flexed had this potent desire moving through her, and she actually felt herself taking a step closer to him.

"I'm glad you said something."

"Callie, there can't ever be anything between us." He scrubbed a hand over his hair and breathed out. "Being with you would mean I'd have to cross a dangerous line, and I can't do that no matter how much I want you." His voice broke on the last word.

Her heart was thundering in her chest. Beads of sweat covered the valley between her breasts, and she could only think about being with him. He said they couldn't be anything together, that being with her was a line he wasn't going to cross, and she knew he was right. But he had said he wanted her, and she wanted him. Something inside of her snapped, and she moved toward him without thinking about anything else aside from being with Lucien. She was close enough to touch him, but he was a big man, at least eight inches taller than her five-foot-seven height.

Callie breathed heavily, feeling herself grow dizzy from the need to touch him.

"Callie, what are you doing?" His voice was deep and husky, and slightly hoarse.

"I don't know, Lucien." She saw him glance down at her mouth, and she licked her lips. She couldn't stop herself, couldn't hold her emotions in check when there was all this sexual chemistry. It was like a living entity between them, and moving back and forth until she was drowning in it, suffocating from the intensity of it. Her hands were shaking, but she lifted them and placed her open palms right on his hard chest. His skin was warm and smooth, hard and powerful. He had his fingers on her wrists, wrapped gently around the bone, but didn't push her away. He flexed his fingers around her, almost like he wanted to send her away from him, but was unable to.

"Callie, I can't do this," he said, but his voice was still hoarse, and his focus was on her lips. "We can't do this," he said even lower, harsher.

"I know, Lucien, but you're all I've been able to think about since that night you took me back to your place when I was drunk, keeping me safe, and not telling my father because I asked you not to."

"Callie." He groaned out almost as if he were in pain. "Goddammit—"

She didn't let him speak anymore, just rose up on her toes, braced her weight with her hands still on his chest, and placed her lips on his. Callie didn't apply pressure, but the electricity that slammed into her when she had her mouth on his was so intense that she actually moaned softly. Lucien still had a hold of her wrists, but he smoothed his big, calloused and rough palms up her arms, and grabbed her shoulders now. For a few seconds, they held their position. But then he pushed her back, and the look on his face had humiliation filling her. He looked pissed, torn, and like the kiss they had just shared hadn't meant anything. Now she felt like a fool, because kissing him had put this huge brick between them. Callie didn't know what to say, didn't know if she should just turn and put all of this behind her. But she knew she couldn't leave things in this awkward moment. "Lucien, I didn't mean to—"

But before she could finish what she was going to say Lucien was right in front of her, his hand behind her head, and his face right in front of hers. "I wanted to stay away, forced myself to stay away because that is the best thing for both of us."

"Lucien." She didn't know what she was going to tell him, but maybe if she explained that this wasn't a passing emotion for her, and that she cared for him more than she had ever cared for another man, he'd know this was worth the risk? "I don't want you to think this isn't real for me." His face was still so close to hers, and his warm breath smelling slightly of whiskey moved across her lips. She swallowed again, felt her nipples bead, and had wetness coating her between her thighs. Her heart would speed up and slow slightly, and repeated the process with each passing second.

"*Fuck*, Callie. This isn't something I can do with you—"

"But you want to do it," she said breathlessly, and cut him off. Callie didn't even want to think about what he might say, and how he might tell her that she needed to leave. Of course that would have been the smart thing for her to do, but right now she didn't want to think about being smart.

"Wanting you and *having* you are two very different things." He searched her face with his gaze, and then moved them back until there wasn't anywhere else for her to go. "But yeah, I fucking want you, have wanted you since I brought you back to my place after you got sick at that party. But I can't have you, Callie, because it's wrong, so fucking wrong, and a betrayal to a man I consider a brother."

"Lucien, how do you think I feel? Kink is my dad." She stared into his silver-grey eyes, and wanted to lean up and kiss him so badly. He didn't say anything, although he still held onto the back of her head. "I love you, Lucien."

God, why had she said that? Why had she said she said she loved him when it was clear he didn't want to take this any further?

"Dammit, Callie, you can't say things like that."

"But why? It's the truth," she said on a whisper, not sure why she was still speaking, because she was just making this worse. Callie should have never come here, should have never gotten out of her car, come to him, and kissed him like some immature and naive child.

He didn't respond, but looked so damn conflicted that her embarrassment consumed her. She felt her face grow hot, knew it was red like a tomato, and wished the ground would open up and swallow her.

"Okay, then maybe I should go, because this was a bad idea." She no longer had her hands on his chest, but she lifted them up again, placed them on his firm pecs, and glanced at his MC patch tattoo. She traced the lines of the silhouetted motorcycle with her gaze, looked at the phoenix that was behind the bike, and it felt like her heart was about to explode in her chest.

I want you, Lucien. God, I want you so bad it hurts.

"You can't say things like that because I am so fucking wrong for you, baby."

Her knees shook at the endearment.

"I am a bad man, Callie, dangerous and far too old for you."

"I don't care about any of that, Lucien."

He leaned in, and she held her breath. He moved his hand from behind her head, cupped the side of her neck, and moved his thumb along her pulse point beneath her ear.

"You should," he said huskily. Lucien lifted his hand and ran his thumb along the top of her lip, just barely touching her, and making her entire body light up with tingles. "You should be so damn afraid of me, running in the other direction, and finding a guy at school that wears cardigans and loafers, not with one who wears leather, and kills men with his bare hands for fucking with him or what he holds close." He slipped his thumb to the seam of her lips now, and without thinking she opened her mouth and sucked his finger inside. "And I'd kill for you, Callie, break a motherfucker in two if they so much as touched you, because I hold you close." Lucien's nostrils flared, and he lowered his eyelids as he watched her mouth. Callie had never been this bold, least of all with a man that lived life on the edge.

And then he was removing his finger from her mouth and was kissing her hard and possessively. For the first time in her life she actually felt the power behind a man kissing *her*. The action was filled with heat, power, and so much sexual tension that she couldn't help but moan against his mouth. He speared his tongue out, slipped it along her bottom lip, and then groaned out loud. Callie had never heard a sound so arousing, but hearing Lucien's desire for her expressed in both sounds and words had her so damn wet she felt her panties became uncomfortably saturated. She grew bold, slid her hand between their bodies, and placed it right over his jean-clad cock.

He groaned low in his throat and pressed his lower body into her belly, which had her back slamming even harder against the wall. But it was the feel of his erection prodding her stomach that had her breaking away from his mouth and gasping out in shock. He was a big man, strong and tall, and she felt like she was so small compared to him. Never had she felt like she was tiny, not with her wide hips and the size sixteen waist, or her thighs that were a bit too thick for her liking.

Lucien stared right into her eyes and didn't move away. She could still feel how hard and big he was between his legs, and she couldn't help but think about what it would feel to have him over her for the first time, taking her virginity and making her feel so stretched she thought she'd split right in two. She knew it would be intense and all consuming, and that she'd never think about any other guy so passionately again.

"Does this tell you how much I want you?" He ground himself against her, and then dipped his head low to run his tongue along her bottom lip. "Does this show you that I am doing something that will get me killed, but that I can't control myself?" he said softly and moved his mouth to her throat.

"Then be with me, Lucien." Callie held onto her shoulders, pressed her breasts to his chest, and kissed his thick, muscular neck. God, he smelled so good, so masculine, and she was about ready to tear her clothes off right now and give herself to him.

He cupped her cheeks and leaned back to look into her face. For several long seconds neither said anything, but they were both breathing heavily, the sexual tension filling the room and making her high and drunk all in the same breath.

And then Lucien exhaled and moved back. The sudden rush of coldness that engulfed her had her bracing her hands on the wall behind her so she didn't fall.

"You need to go, Callie." Lucien glanced away.

She saw that he was still so hard, his erection pressing against his fly, but he kept moving back from her. "Lucien, we don't have to stop."

The look he gave her had her tensing. His expression was so distant and hard, so unwavering, that she felt so very out of place right now. Gone was the arousal she'd felt just seconds before, and in its place was this icy realization that the Lucien that had just been touching and kissing her was no longer in front of her. Right now it was the fierce Brothers of Menace President who killed men with his bare hands.

"Go, Callie." He ran his hand over his hair, turned around so his back was to her, and she saw his muscles go tense. "You need to go before I do something I'll

regret, and before I betray Kink and have him hating me."
He didn't turn around, but she felt the truth in his words.

"I don't want to hurt my dad either, Lucien, but I
love you." She felt her humiliation take a back seat in this
situation as her passion and her words took the front.
"Doesn't that mean anything to you?"

He turned around, and the fierceness on his face
had her swallowing hard. "Don't my feelings, or the fact
you want me, mean anything to you?" she asked.

He took a step toward her. "It means a fucking lot,
but I can't be with a member's daughter, Callie. It would
mean war, hate, and a whole lot of fucking violence." He
stepped closer, and she felt the heat from his body slam
into her. "I can't be that selfish, and I can't put you and
Kink in the middle of all of this. It isn't right, Callie."

She knew this, but didn't want to hear it. She had
put herself and her feelings out there. He had let her
sample it, let her love grow for those few seconds, and
then he had shut her down. She knew that being with
Lucien might hurt and anger her father, but for once in
her life she wanted something bad enough that she would
have dealt with the consequence and tried to make them
right after the fact.

"You're right." Being selfish certainly wasn't a
trait Callie practiced, but she had also never been in love
before.

"Callie…" he said in a gruff, pained voice.

She shook her head and turned to move toward
the door. She couldn't look at him, and couldn't think
about the fact her lips still tingled from their kiss.
Running out of the clubhouse seemed like the best option
because the embarrassment and hurt that filled her had
her wanting to escape. She didn't want to stay here and to
make an even bigger ass out of herself. She just needed to
go, and put this behind her like she had planned from the

beginning. The only one that would end up getting hurt was her, and she was already sampling that pain right now. If she didn't leave now she didn't know if she'd be able to handle anymore.

****

Lucien stared at the bedroom door where Callie had just left. Self-anger and hatred grew inside of him, and he felt himself grow even tenser. He curled his hand into a tight fist and slammed it into the wall. The plaster crumbled all around his hand, and the hole in the wall spoke of his pain. He had just kissed Kink's daughter, told her he wanted her, and had ground his fucking erection into her belly like she was experienced in all of this. Although sending her away was the smart thing to do, he was too late in it all, wanted her like a fucking fiend, and knew that staying away at this point would be the hardest thing he had ever done. The taste of her filled his mouth, and her scent, a light and floral aroma, filled his head. He was drunk from her, needed to get off so badly that he felt like a crazy beast, but knew that his suffering was justified.

Looking down at his fist, he saw the broken skin and watched as blood trailed along his fingers. He went over to his disassembled gun lying on the table, and growled out. He needed to go shoot something, maybe go out in the middle of the fucking woods and pop some bullets in tree trunks. He needed something to burn off this wild, nervous energy, and this angry hatred he had inside of himself for his stupid actions.

"You stupid fucking asshole," he said to himself, and walked over to the window. He watched as Callie got into her car, stared at the clubhouse for a second, and then shook her head. She was saying something to herself, maybe chastising herself over the fact they kissed, or the fact that he was a bastard and she was better off without him in her life. The latter would have been true.

She finally left, and Lucien stared at where her car had been parked. With each passing second he grew angrier with himself, wished things could be different so he could be with Callie, and then he just exploded in a torrent of emotion. He slammed his fist into the wall over and over, felt his knuckles crack open even more and blood slide down his hand, but relished the pain. He was going to kill someone if they came in here right now, if they approached him and started asking questions about what was up with him. And the longer he stayed at the clubhouse the sooner someone would come back and do just that.

He grabbed his keys and shirt, and once he was fully dressed he headed out of the clubhouse and to his Harley. He didn't care where he was heading, as long as it was away from this fucking place.

Chapter Four

Callie drove to Baker University, which was a good three hours away from River Run. Despite the nervousness of starting her life alone for the first time, the incident at the clubhouse with Lucien, and the fact that she was still humiliated, depressed, and angry because of the kiss and her emotions, she was trying to think about the future. This was only the weekend where she would get to see her dorm, have a tour of the campus, and, she hoped, meet some people before school started. It was a new program they had started, one where she would be busy all weekend, and even get to stay in her dorm. Although Lucien's words slammed into her head, reminding her that she could never really be with him no matter how much she loved him, she didn't even want to think about her life with another guy. Yes, she was young, had the whole world in front of her, but Lucien was different. She certainly knew that she couldn't just forget him no matter what he or she said.

Putting her thoughts of River Run and Lucien behind her, she focused on the road ahead of her. She saw the university about half an hour later, and her nerves grew to the point she was suffocating on it. The buildings were so big and intimidating, and she felt like this little bee in a massive hive that would eat her alive. Although she knew there was something very profound about taking the next step in her life, fear was paramount inside of her. The bone searing terror that she felt at that exact moment was not something they'd warned her about in the welcome letter.

She parked her car, got her lone bag out of the backseat, and stared at the building in front of her. The deep breath she took should have calmed her, but all she felt was tightness in her chest. Students moved in and out of the propped open doorway of the admin building. She was to meet here and given her dorm information, but she was frozen to the spot, not knowing where to go or what to do.

"You look lost." The male voice behind her had Callie looking over her shoulder. The guy standing just a foot from her looked like one of those models that had their image splashed across GQ magazines. Totally not her type, but still gorgeous, and smiling at her like a boy-next-door.

"I guess I am, that or like I'm making an ass out of myself." She could have slapped her hand over her mouth. God, she had really just tried to crack a joke. A total nervous thing she did on occasion, but she was thankful the guy started laughing.

"Beautiful and a sense of humor. You'll fit right in," he said, and she felt her face heat. She wasn't used to compliments. Callie was used to being around gruff and alpha bikers, not guys that had blond hair perfectly styled, wearing designer looking jeans and a button down shirt, and smelling like he was wearing really expensive cologne. She liked the scent of clean sweat and motor oil, liked a man in worn, dirty jeans because he had been fixing his Harley, and she especially liked them covered in tattoos.

You're describing Lucien, Callie. You need to try to focus on the here and now, because Lucien made himself clear. Besides, do you really want Dad and Lucien to be on the outs because you couldn't help your emotions?

No.

Already she felt out of place, but right now, as she stared at this Adonis looking guy, she felt like she had been dropped in The Twilight Zone. She knew that with time things would become more comfortable … or at least that was what she kept telling herself.

"Don't worry, everyone feels scared shitless on their first day," he said, his grin wide. "I'm Ritchie Mitchell by the way." He held out his hand, and she glanced down at it. "I'm originally from Broomfield. You?" His fingernails looked perfectly manicured, and his skin was soft and golden in color. Yeah, he had never worked with his hands, clearly. She took his hand with her free one, and just like her prior observation, smooth skin greeted her.

"Callie Roberts from River Run."

"Here, let me take that for you, and then I'll show you where you can get your dorm number and welcome packet." He took the bag out of her hand before she could respond, and then gestured for her to follow him.

Callie moved past two students hauling big ass suitcases out of the admin building. The inside of the admin building opened up, showing skylights and a cathedral ceiling in the center of the room. There were several tables lined up, each one having a sign hanging in front of them and directing students to different stations.

Schedules, dorm assignments, welcome packets, activity lists, and general information were a few of the first tables that students were lining up in front of. After about twenty-five minutes she had all the papers and headed back outside. Ritchie had stayed by her the entire time, and she was grateful that he had walked her through it, and had also been able to get in the front of the lines so she wasn't waiting in line for the next hour.

Ritchie started talking about the different sights around town, of the sororities that she could join—which she didn't bother telling him that she didn't plan on getting involved with—and took her to the Stanford East dorm building. It was like he was Callie's own personal tour guide. She didn't know if she should be thankful for the fact he took an interest in helping a stranger, or feel a little embarrassed at the fact she had looked so helpless.

Students packed the halls of Stanford Hall East, and she had to continuously excuse herself as they loitered around. Once she made it to her room, Ritchie stood by the open doorway and handed her bag.

"Well, this is you." He grinned. "And actually I am just a few doors down."

She glanced at him, a little surprised. "Really? What are the odds of that?"

He shrugged and pushed off the doorway, but he was still ginning. "If you need anything just let me know, but I'll let you get settled in." He went to turn away, but stopped and grabbed the doorframe. He stared at her and tapped his fingers on the wood.

"Hey, if you're all settled later on tonight, there is a party at the frat house I am with. You can meet a lot of students from the college, drink a little, and socialize." He lifted a brow now, kept smiling, and she knew that if she was going to make this whole college thing work she needed to get out there and make some friends. She also wanted to party, because as it was she felt strung-out from the incident just this morning with Lucien.

"Yeah, okay." She smiled in return and placed her bag on one of the two beds.

"Sweet. I'll come by about eight to take you there." He tapped on the frame once more, and then left her alone.

She walked over to the door and watched as he stopped and spoke to a few guys before heading to his room down the hall.

She stood there for a full minute and looked around. The room was on the bigger side, with a small bathroom and even a kitchenette with one of those mini fridges. There were two twin beds, a couple of dressers, some shelving drilled into the white painted cement blocks, and a small window between the beds. When she walked toward the window she saw the front of the campus, could see the main office, Brown Hall, the library, and even the admin building.

"At least you have a view."

Over the next few weeks she'd have to bring her things up here, but aside from clothes, a few personal items, and maybe her books, she didn't have anything of importance that needed to be with her here. After staring out the window for a few more seconds she sat on the bed, took her cell out, and dialed her dad. He had wanted to take her to campus, but she'd said she could do it alone, and needed to be able to stand on her own while out here. Since her mom died her dad had been tiptoeing around her, feeling like maybe he couldn't be himself. She assumed as much, gauged that was what he might be feeling because of the way he looked at her with this almost sad expression. She sighed and dialed his number, and put the phone to her ear. It only rang twice before her dad picked up.

"Hey, sweetheart," Kink said in a deep, gravelly voice, and the sound of rock music could be heard. She assumed her dad was working on his bike or some kind of vehicle, and when she heard the clank of something hard and metal hitting something else equally hard and possibly metal, she knew that was what he was doing.

"Keeping busy so I don't freak out and head back home."

The sound of the music lowering and of her father breathing out came through the receiver.

"Honey, you don't have to go to that school. You can go to one closer where you can still stay with Cookie and me at the house." The silence stretched between them for a second. "I want you to experience life, but I also want you to be comfortable. With everything that has happened these last few months I don't want you to be stressing yourself unnecessarily."

"I'm fine, Dad, really." She glanced down at her hands, her gaze locked on her fingers as she picked at a loose thread on her shirt. She thought about Lucien, about everything that they had done, and wondered what he was doing now. Was he searching for one of those easy club girls to ease the blue balls he had to have? She didn't know if he was still sleeping with them, even though he was barely on the mend, and the fact that she knew he had feelings for her. The problem was she didn't know how deep his feelings for her were, and thinking about him having sex with anyone, least of all those loose girls they always seemed to have at the clubhouse, made her ill.

"Met anyone yet?"

"Dad, I've been here like an hour total." She glanced at the door, and remembered Ritchie's help. "Actually, I did meet a guy, a really nice one that helped me with getting my information packets and even showed me my dorm." The line got deathly quiet. "Dad?"

"He try anything on you?"

"What?" She stared at the wall in front of her and started chuckling. "Dad, he's like an advisor or something, and totally just showed me where things were."

"Uh huh, well if he touches you in any way that is inappropriate then you tell me and I'll rip his balls off—"

"Dad, please don't go all alpha biker on the situation."

"Okay, okay, but I want to make sure my daughter is okay."

"I'm okay, Dad, and in fact going to some kind of social tonight."

"Social, like a party?"

"Yeah, Dad, but everything is okay. I'm not a baby anymore."

He exhaled. "I know, darlin'. I worry though."

She smiled at his concern. Even though she liked speaking to him, loved that he was worried because he cared about her, she felt guilt every time they spoke. Callie wanted to tell him about how she felt for Lucien, but the more time that passed the more she knew she never would say anything to her dad. She should have just told him right away, but with it now being months away she knew even if he hadn't freaked out if she would have told him then, he most definitely would now.

"Be careful, Callie, and call me when you get back, no matter the time."

They spoke for another five minutes, and she finally got off the phone, set it on the bed beside her, and lay back. She stared at the off white ceiling, thought about what trouble she could get into this weekend, but knew she would probably be moping around. Nothing like having one's hopes shot down by the man she loved to put someone in a shitty mood.

"Hey, watch it, prick."

The voice coming from down the hall drew Callie's attention. Before she even entered the room she knew that coarse language had to be coming from her roommate. At least she hoped so. Callie wanted to be shacked up with someone that wasn't a pushover, and had some life. However, she had heard horror stories from Ian's older brother about his freshman year and the roommate he had gotten stuck with.

When the young girl rounded the corner and stepped into the room Callie pushed herself up on the bed and braced her upper bodyweight on her elbows. The first thought that came to Callie's mind was that she was bunking with a Gypsy. The girl who she presumed was her roomie had hair that was a wild mass of black curls that fell down her back. The sound of her twenty bangle bracelets jangling against her wrists preceded each step she took. Her multicolored ankle length skirt swirled around her as she literally sashayed across the threshold. She was very pretty, with an ethnic flare to her that instantly had Callie admiring every part of her.

"Oh hey," the girl said and stopped by Callie's feet. "You must be my roomie." She said it without question, and Callie should have been offended by the way she eyed her up and down. But her warm smile made it hard to feel that way. She offered her hand to Callie, and she stood and took the offered gesture.

"I'm Meredith Jacobson." The girl dropped Callie's hand and tossed her bag onto the free bed. She turned around with a brow raised and stared at Callie. "Do you have a name or should I just call you girl?" She was teasing. Callie could tell in her voice and see it in the smile she offered.

"Callie Roberts." She smiled at Meredith. "I'm not usually this spazzy, I swear."

Meredith laughed and lifted her hand as if to brush her comment aside. "No worries. I was just giving you a hard time." She turned and started tossing her clothes out of her duffle. The sound of her bangle brackets jingling on her wrists seemed to fill the room and kept Callie in a kind of trance.

Callie sat back on the bed and grabbed a sweater out of her bag. "Where are you from, Meredith?"

"Originally Utah, but we moved to Colorado when I was I fourth grade. My parents are set up in Northglenn." She looked over her shoulder. "You?"

"River Run."

"Dang, I think I've heard about that place." Meredith sat on the bed and knitted her brows. "Was that where that big ass explosion happened, or where all those dead cult people bodies were found?"

"How sad is it that you know the town from the news?" Callie chuckled, but it was dry and not very humorous. "But the explosion was in Steel Corner, the town right beside River Run, which is where the cult issues were at."

"Damn," Meredith said. "You're not one of those biker princesses, are you?"

Callie chuckled, and this time there was amusement in the tone. "There really is no such thing as biker princesses, but my dad is the VP of a club."

"*Shiiiiit*," Meredith said seriously. "You must be hardcore then?"

"Um, me?" Callie shook her head and chuckled. "The most hardcore I ever got was getting trashed at a party, and calling my then-boyfriend and the whore he had cheated on me with a bunch of names."

Meredith grinned wider. "Yeah, you are totally my kind of roomie. So, what's your major?" Meredith turned back to grab a few more things out of her bag.

"I don't actually know, really."

Meredith laughed. "Hey, you're entitled to be undecided your first year. Just don't let it carry over after that or you become one of *those* students."

"One of those students?" Callie leaned back and rested her upper body on her elbows again.

"Yeah, one of those students that are in college for like six years, but could have graduated two years before that. One of those students that enjoys the college life way too much to actually grow up." Meredith tossed her hair over her shoulder and watched Callie intently.

"You have a major?" Callie asked.

"Holistic Healing is my ultimate goal, but right now I am taking all the bullshit classes: biology, chemistry, English Comp, stuff like that. Once I get the first couple of years under my belt and have the pre-req stuff done I'll get into meditation, some medical classes, and then some of the more holistic courses." Meredith sounded very passionate about her goals, and Callie wished she were there in her life, too.

"So, you got rid of the douchebag cheating ex, but another boyfriend in the background?" Meredith asked, but she was looking at her phone now.

"Ugh, no boyfriend in the woodwork."

Meredith stopped typing on her phone and glanced up. For a second she didn't say anything, and then she grinned.

"What?" Callie asked and straightened.

"That tone you just had, that totally means you got one on the side." She grinned. "Let me guess, because, girl, I am good at reading between the lines, and the fact your face is red as hell tells me there is more to the story."

Callie felt her face heat and knew that even if she hadn't gotten embarrassed Meredith was clearly the type of person that could hear what wasn't being said. But who was Callie kidding? She had Lucien on the brain, and clearly that wasn't hard to pick up on.

"No, there isn't more to the story." Callie cleared her throat. Meredith's gaze was unmoving, and she glanced away, needing to focus on something aside from this girl she had just met, but who clearly knew more about her than she had told anyone else.

"I'm sorry. I'm known to be nosy and assume shit." Meredith smiled, but it was soft and apologetic.

Callie shrugged. "It's nothing, but I don't want to talk about it, if that makes sense."

Meredith smiled. "It's nothing, but you don't want to talk about it means it is something, but I feel ya, girl. Consider it dropped unless you ever want to talk. Then I'm here." Meredith fell back on the bed. She closed her eyes and put her hands above her head.

"You see the hotties that live down the hall?" Meredith said but didn't open her eyes or move. "I swear it is like a sausage factory on our floor. We lucked out, Callie." Meredith smiled widely, but still didn't look at Callie.

"I actually didn't have a lot of time to check anyone out, although I will say the guy that showed me around and has a room right down the hall was really nice."

Meredith did sit up then, and she cocked a dark arched eyebrow. "Yeah? Sounds like I might need some help, and he could be the person to lend a hand."

"He invited me to a frat party tonight at eight." Now it was Callie's turn to lift an eyebrow. "I told him I'd go, but honestly I probably would have bitched out anyway. But if you go I'd check it out, meet some people, maybe even get familiar with the area." Memories of her partying, drunken encounter months ago, and Lucien coming to save the day, were still very much fresh in her mind. She had agreed out of courtesy, told her dad even, but the truth was she probably would have declined when the time came to go.

"Yeah?" Meredith flipped her hair over her shoulder. "Girl, I am there."

"I have to go to this freshman orientation thing at noon." Callie wasn't really looking forward to being tied up all day with what would be boring statistics of the university, the founders, and probably a lot of other administration points, but she had come here to get acquainted with everything.

"I'm all tied up, too, but I don't think we are in the same group since mine starts at two." Meredith stood and took out her phone from her bag when it started ringing. "Hey, it's my mom, and if I don't take it she'll freak," Meredith said and gave her this sympathetic smile. "Hey Mom, hold on." She pulled the phone away and covered the mouthpiece. "I'm sorry." She smiled. "But I am totally here for the frat party. But we stick together, well, unless I hook it up, girl," Meredith said softly and winked. Callie couldn't tell if she was being serious. "I'll be back at the dorm at like six-ish? I have some paperwork to fill out for my financial aid."

Callie nodded, and Meredith turned and headed for the bathroom. Meredith started speaking to her mother in a different language, and the sound of her bangle bracelets jangled until she shut the bathroom door behind her. Callie turned and focused on the window again, and then fell back on the bed, closed her eyes, and then thought about the life she was about to lead, the journey she would take, and the fact she could do this without having Lucien in her life the way she wanted.

Things didn't always work out the way someone wanted, and if she thought about it constantly she would be stuck, covered in her desires that would never be a reality and she didn't want to live that way. She could do this, could see Lucien down the road and not have to feel this longing for him, and thinking maybe one day things would work out for her. She could look at him and see the President of The Brothers of Menace, and nothing more.

Looking up at the ceiling, she knew that all of that was nothing but a load of bullshit.

Chapter Five

Lucien stepped into the clubhouse, his hand busted up and bandaged, his body achy from the workout he had done earlier in the day, and the need to get a good buzz on riding him hard. He still had the flavor of Callie on his lips even all these hours later, still had the tingle from their kiss moving through his veins, and didn't fucking like it because he felt off balance and unstable. He had worked out so damn hard his muscles ached, he had sweated so much he had gotten dehydrated, and then he had jerked off in the shower thinking of Callie. But having his cock in his palm, his other hand braced on the wall, and his head lowered with his eyes closed as he thought about her, made him feel like a sick bastard. The things he had thought about, pictured doing with Callie, had gotten him off so damn quick. Her naked before him, her lush body on full display, her tits and pussy begging for his mouth and hands. Yeah, he had come hard enough that his legs had shaken from the force of it.

Sleeping for a few hours hadn't cleared his head, and he was right back where he had been before he had grown exhausted. Now he was at the clubhouse, ready to get his drink on, smoke some pot, too, and he hoped get through this bump in his life.

He saw Cookie and Kink at the bar and knew he shouldn't go by the VP because he was feeling like a bastard, but then Kink waved him over.

"Hey, man," Kink said when Lucien came closer.

"Hey." Lucien tapped on the bar and ordered a beer from the prospect.

"You doing okay?" Kink asked.

Lucien glanced at the other man, and saw the flash of what he had done with his VP's daughter just earlier that day, and shook his head to clear it. "I'm good, brother. You doing good? You look like you're on top of the world."

Kink grinned and pulled Cookie close to him. "I am, brother."

Lucien took the beer from the prospect, and turned around to lean back on the bar. "I'm glad through all the shit that had gone down with the club that something good came out of it." He stared at the scene before him, of his guys having a good time, getting drunk, smoking weed to unwind, and enjoying the women that were grinding on them like they were trying to get the members' cocks to tear through their jeans. And from past experience Lucien knew the club pussy women could get a cock harder than granite—well, they used to be able to get his cock that hard. Now the damn fucker stayed limp unless it was Callie on his mind.

"Yeah, just goes to show you that some happiness can come to a bastard like me," Kink said and started chuckling. "We just came by so Cookie could drop off some paperwork for Tatum, but then all these assholes started coming up and talking to us, and then we started drinking," Kink looked at Cookie and smiled. "Anyway, things are getting wild here, and I want to be alone with my woman." Kink looked back at Lucien. "If I don't occupy myself with something I'll just be worrying about Callie all damn weekend."

Lucien strained and faced Kink. "Why? Everything okay with her?" He felt on edge even more now at the thought of Callie in trouble, but then he told himself that she was safe in the dorm room, and that Kink's worrying was what a devoted father did.

Kink waved off his questions. "She's good, just left for that orientation thing at the university. She'll be back tomorrow evening, but still, stresses the fuck out of me."

Lucien relaxed. "She leave already, huh?" he said, his voice a bit strained, and for the first time in his life he felt pretty fucking uncomfortable in front of one of his members. Yeah, he knew Callie had left, because he had kissed her right before he told her to leave.

Kink nodded. "I swear I'll be worrying about her so fucking much I'm liable to age a decade by the time she comes home for a break."

Cookie started chuckling. "Kink, she'll be fine. It's only for a few days, and then she'll be back where you can be the overprotective papa bear."

Kink scoffed. "Baby, she will still have to go back in a couple of fucking weeks." Kink scrubbed a hand over his face and breathed out. "Lucien, man, be glad you don't have a daughter that is going to college, hanging out at those fucking frat parties, and probably having assholes sniff around her."

Lucien straightened at the mention of a frat party. "She's going to parties already?"

Kink shrugged. "She mentioned going to one of them tonight. She's a good girl, and I trust her to take care of herself, but man, thinking of all those pricks hanging around her." Kink shook his head. "They are the ones I don't trust.

Yeah, Lucien didn't trust those little assholes either, because he had been one years ago, knew how they thought, and knew that all they had on their minds was getting their dicks wet. All Lucien could think about was the shit that had almost happened to her all those months ago when she had gone to a party. What if one of those motherfuckers drugged her drink, tried something on her, and he wasn't able to take care of her like last time? Why in the hell would she put herself in that situation again? He was starting to get pissed, visualizing all the fucking shit that could go wrong, and feeling like an asshole for pushing her aside. But when he looked at Kink he saw the other man watching him curiously.

"You doing okay, man? You look like someone sucker punched you and you're about to go ape-shit."

Lucien exhaled roughly, turned away from Kink to stare at the club, and then ran a hand over his scruff-covered cheeks. When he looked at Kink again he smiled, knew it was fake as fuck, but was not about to do this now. He had Callie on his mind, those horrible images of her alone at that party, fuckers trying to take advantage of her, and couldn't think straight. Lucien saw red, saw bodies at his feet as he kicked every asshole that talked to her, and had to leave now. He knew what he had to do, because if he didn't he'd be a motherfucking mess and start destroying shit.

****

The music was loud and pulsing, and the number of bodies crammed into this two-story house was intense. Callie had been at the frat party for the last couple of hours, and aside from the lone beer she had drunk an hour ago, she was now sticking with bottled water. It was hot as hell in the house, and sweat beaded between her breasts and along the length of her spine. Meredith was beside her talking to a guy she apparently knew from high school, and the vibes Meredith and the guy were throwing off to each other were nauseating and way too damn sexual for Callie's liking.

"Hey, I'm going to get some fresh air," Callie said, having to yell over the music.

Meredith turned and shook her head. "No, we don't leave without the other even for some air. I'll just have Brandon come with us?"

Now it was Callie's turn to shake her head. "I kind of am not feeling the whole fuck me vibe I'm getting from you two." Callie grinned. "Besides, I'll just be right outside on the porch. It is hot, and I'm sweaty."

Meredith shook her head again.

It was nice that, although she had just met Meredith, she felt like they were already good friends. She was about to tell her that she'd be fine ten feet away, but Ritchie's voice came through the loud music, and was right by her ear.

"Want to be my chaperone outside?"

She looked at him and smiled. He smiled back, held up a bottle of unopened beer, and pointed to the front door.

She turned and looked at Meredith. "See, I have someone now to watch over me, and now you'll be able to properly catch up with Brandon and give each other the 'fuck me eyes'" Callie nudged her in the shoulder. Meredith glanced at Brandon, grinned, and then nodded at her, so Callie moved away from the wall they had been standing by and toward the front door. Once outside, there was a handful of people loitering around the porch, smoking cigarettes, drinking beer, and tossing the cups aside. Callie and Ritchie moved to the back of the porch where no one was, and she pressed her back to the railing.

"Thanks for getting me out of there. I know Meredith wanted to talk with Brandon some more, and I was feeling like a third wheel."

Ritchie handed her the beer, and she shook her head. She held up her bottle of water. "Thanks but no thanks."

He shrugged and set the bottle on the ledge, then leaned on the railing, too. After Ritchie took a swig from his bottle he glanced at her. "So Meredith knows that guy in there?"

Callie nodded. "Yeah, I guess they were kind of close in high school, like that friends with benefits kind of close." She smiled and then chuckled when Ritchie's eyebrows rose.

"Wow, can't say I've ever had that kind of friendship."

Callie chuckled harder. "Yeah, me either." *Hell, I have never had any kind of sexual relationship for that matter.* Of course that was a piece of information she wasn't about to share with him. "Hey, thanks again for taking us here tonight. I met some really great people-even a few that are in my courses."

"Glad no one was a douchebag to you. Some of the guys can get … touchy-feely when they are drunk and there are pretty girls around." He looked at her out of the corner of his eyes.

She felt her face heat, and although it was dark and she knew he probably couldn't see how he had embarrassed her with his compliment, she didn't doubt he probably could guess by the way she shifted on her feet.

"Well, I'm glad none of them were douchey, and if they had gotten touchy-feely I would have kicked them in the balls."

Ritchie started laughing hard. "That's a girl. Kick them where it counts. Remind me never to get on your bad side." He reached out, and before she knew what he was doing he pushed a piece of her hair off her shoulder. "Your hair is really soft," he said softly and looked at her right in the eyes. "You have a boyfriend, Callie?" he asked, looking at her lips now.

"I, uh—" She felt really uncomfortable right now, yet she couldn't see to move as her surprise at what was happening moved through her. "No, I don't have a boyfriend, but—"

"No boyfriend, but you're so pretty." He cut her off and leaned in, and the scent of his beer breath moved along her face.

Callie moved away before his lips touched hers, and she cleared her throat in discomfort. "Um, Ritchie." She faced him, saw that he was looking a little uncomfortable, and smiled softly. "I'm not really looking for anything like that right now." She ran her hands on her thighs and told herself she could have used a beer right now, but then thought better of it.

"Nah, it was my fault for reading something that wasn't there, and for thinking I could be so bold." He laughed, but it was clearly awkward. "I'm kind of drunk, and was not thinking clearly." He rubbed his face with his hand and then finished off his beer. He grabbed the unopened one he had brought for her, popped the cap, and then downed that one, too.

"Hey, no worries." She didn't want either of them to be uncomfortable, and when he chuckled again she felt the weirdness in the air start to leave.

"Okay, don't mind me, and please let's forget all the stupid shut I just did and said right now?" He looked hopeful.

"Of course." She smiled, feeling better already. She may have only met Ritchie, but he had been really nice to her, showed her around when he didn't have to, and having him turn out to be an asshole would have been shitty.

The sound of a motorcycle engine revving had her heart racing and her looking toward the street. Of course she knew it wouldn't be Lucien, but it was kind of second nature for her brain to jump to the conclusion that it was the man she craved. It was also instant to have the image of him on that massive motorcycle filling her head, making her hot that had nothing to do with the party, and to feel sensitive all over.

"Hey, you mind if I grab another beer?" Ritchie said, oblivious to the fact she was searching the street like some kind of psycho, looking for someone that would clearly not be there.

She shook her head and glanced at him. "Of course not, I'm not going anywhere without Meredith." She looked in the window beside her and could see Meredith sitting on the couch with Brandon. He had his hand over her shoulder and was playing with a piece of her hair. "And I don't think I'll be going anywhere for a while."

Ritchie nodded, and then lifted up the now two empty beer bottles. "You sure you're good on the drink department?"

She held up her bottle of water and nodded. "I'm good, thank you."

He turned and went inside, pushed through the throng of people standing by the front door, and then disappeared. She turned and focused on the street again, feeling stupid for even thinking about Lucien. She should purge him from her mind and forget about everything she felt, but of course that was easier said than done. And then she exhaled, leaned on the railing, and stared at the cars parked in front of the house. But it was the flash of silver right under the street lamp at the corner of the street that caught her eye. She followed her gaze up the big front wheel, over the gleaming chrome and detailed custom work, and the stopped when she saw the thick, big hands that held onto the handlebars. Her heart started working double time, her palms started sweating, and she knew without a doubt that she wasn't seeing things.

Lucien Silver was here, sitting on his Harley just feet from where she stood, and staring right at her.

Chapter Six

No, Callie was most definitely not seeing things. Lucien was here, at her college and looking like he was about to tear shit up. He wore his leather cut, had on his rugged and worn-in jeans, and the shadows partially covered his face. But Callie knew it was him, could see the way his eerie grey eyes watched her, moved with her actions, and then she found herself moving forward. But a hand on her arm stopped her. She looked back, saw Ritchie handing her a fresh bottle of water. He then followed her gaze to where Lucien sat.

"Hey, you know him?" Ritchie asked, and still had his hand on her arm.

She glanced at Lucien, and her stomach did a flip when she watched him climb off his bike, his face a mask of pure rage as he moved with determined strides toward them. "I do." She pulled her arm out of Ritchie's grasp. "You should go." She tried to get him to leave, because the way Lucien was moving toward them, and the fact he looked pissed as hell, told Callie he was jumping to conclusions about Ritchie touching her.

"I can't leave you when that beast of a guy is barreling toward us."

"He's my dad's friend, but he doesn't look happy, so please, Ritchie, you should go." She pleaded, and then finally he took a step back. He looked between her and then Lucien, and finally turned and headed back to the house, but she could see that he stayed on the porch. It was sweet that he was looking out for her, but against Lucien he was this string-bean of a kid.

She stared at Lucien, and he stopped a few feet from her. He glanced over her shoulder, most likely at Ritchie, and she saw his nostrils flare and his jaw clench.

"What are you doing here?" she asked, still

surprised that Lucien was standing right in front of her. He smelled good, like cologne that was wild and dark, and motor oil from working on his bike. He had on a white shirt under his cut, and she could see the defined outline of his muscles under the thin material. His short dark hair was a disarray around his head, but God, did it look good on him, and his eerie, powerful silver colored eyes watched them both with menace. She felt her arousal and feelings for this man come back with a vengeance. Of course they hadn't disappeared, never would, she knew, but seeing him here in the flesh, hours away from River Run, had her feeling drunk off of the sight of him.

He pulled his focus away from the frat house, but it seemed like it took him a lot of effort. He stared at her, the muscles under his jaw clenching, but the look he gave her, solely her, could have had her melting from the intensity of it if she had been a weaker woman. Hell, who was she kidding? When it came to Lucien she *was* weak.

"Your dad told me you were coming to a party, and all I could think about was the shit you had gotten yourself into three months ago." His voice was hard and unforgiving.

"I'm fine, and am drinking water." She knew that she had been stupid back then at the party Lucien had saved her from, but she had learned her lesson, and was not about to get put into that situation again, especially not one weekend away from home. She crossed her arms over her chest, feeling this chill in the air even though she was still hot. "But to have you ride all the way over here because you thought I'd fuck up again?" She didn't mince her words, and although she was thrilled to see him on a physical and emotional level because of how she felt for him, she was a little annoyed that he had come barreling out of the darkness about to kick Ritchie's ass.

"It isn't you that I'm worried about making mistakes, Callie. You're smart as fuck, and I know you don't put yourself in harm's way purposefully." He tilted his chin toward the frat house. "It's all those motherfuckers in there that have me getting pissed, because I know what is going through their minds when they look at you." He growled out the words and glanced down at her clothes. "I'm glad you're covered up. When that fuck put his hand on you I about lost it, Callie. I saw red and didn't give a shit if I committed murder." He stared at her hard. "I meant it when I said I'd kill if any asshole put their motherfucking hands on you." His voice was a low growl.

His voice was getting harder, darker, and she looked behind her. There were a few people watching them a little apprehensively, but she had a feeling it had to do with the fact Lucien was a scary guy in general, and not the fact that a biker was standing in the yard.

"I'm fine, everything here is fine, and you're causing a scene." She might love him, but right now she was annoyed. Callie grabbed his thickly muscled forearm and pulled him away, but at first it was like trying to move a slab of marble. Finally he relented and allowed her to pull him a few feet away from the house. She moved them over to his bike, glanced at the party again, and then exhaled. "Does my dad know you're here?"

He crossed his arms over his massive and wide chest, and stared down at her. She was not a thin woman by any means, and with a size sixteen waist, boobs that were a little too large for her liking, and curves that she didn't care much for, Lucien still managed to make her feel so feminine and petite.

"What do you think, Callie?"

The way he said her name had a chill and tremor moving through her. That was a no. He had not told her father, and although she was thankful because Kink would have flipped his shit, and because she knew she didn't want anyone's relationship to be strained, she had a feeling things would become that way eventually.

"Lucien, you made yourself clear back at the clubhouse. I left, went away because you told me to. I don't understand why you'd show up, act like you care—"

"I do fucking care." His voice grew harder. "I worried about you, Callie, and the only way I could not lose my shit and destroy something was to come up here and make sure you were okay."

That had her shutting up, swallowing the lump that was suddenly in her throat, and she was stunned that he had said the last part softly, intimately even. The sound of footsteps approaching had Callie turning. Meredith and Brandon were walking toward them, and by the looks on both of their faces it was clear Lucien standing here shocked them. He was intimidating on the best of days, but with his anger still below the surface, and the aura of his dangerous nature simmering so close, she knew anyone within a foot of him could sense how powerful this man really was.

"I, uh, Brandon and I were going to head out for something to eat, and catch up," Meredith said, tripping over her words, but she was staring at Lucien as she spoke. She finally looked at Callie. "You're okay?"

"I'm fine. This is my father's friend, Lucien." She nodded at Lucien.

Meredith eyed him curiously. "Damn, hardcore biker in the flesh." Meredith almost sounded awed, but Brandon looked a little hesitant to even be so close to Lucien. "So you want to go with us, or, uh, something else you have planned?" She eyed Lucien again.

"Actually—"

"I'll just take you back to the dorm, Callie. It's late, and your dad probably would be pissed knowing you're out partying with a bunch of drunk adolescents." He looked at Meredith. "No offense," he said, but he didn't sound very genuine.

She didn't bother saying her dad knew where she was, that she had told him she was going to a frat party. None of it would have mattered when it concerned Lucien wanting something. It was weird hearing Lucien be all responsible sounding, especially as she knew he was less than sedentary when it came to his life and partying. She wanted to argue, to tell him he couldn't just show up and start telling her what she could and couldn't do, but she was ready for this night to be over with, and didn't want to start any more of a scene than Lucien had already caused.

"None taken," Meredith said, and then the sound of someone puking in the not too far distance came through, confirming Lucien's words. Meredith looked over her shoulder, and then when she looked back at them she had this scrunched up nose. "Hence why we are leaving, because the sound and smell of vomit is kind of doing me in." She shrugged. "You're good with going back to the dorm though?" she asked Callie, and eyed Lucien again.

"I was thinking of heading back anyway, and I know you two want to catch up, so it's fine." Callie looked at Lucien, and felt her arousal and annoyance wage war.

"Okay, only if you're sure."

Callie nodded. "I am, but thanks." She smiled, knowing that this whole frat scene wasn't for her anyway. And since Ritchie had tried to kiss her, it was a little uncomfortable.

"Well, don't wait up for me," Meredith said.

"Seriously, I haven't seen this guy in the flesh in forever. He moved away junior year, and seeing him here totally caught me off guard." Meredith was looking at Brandon. Callie didn't know the deal with them, or how they had been friends with benefits but hadn't seen each other in a long time, but she was fine staying in the dark about it all. Meredith nudged Brandon in the ribs, and then they turned and left. The sound of her bangles jangling as she made her way toward her car sounded loud and distinct. When Meredith and Brandon got into the car and drove away, the silence, despite the pounding music coming through the house, surrounded Callie and Lucien.

"Come on, let's go," Lucien said in that hard tone of his, but when she looked at the house she saw Ritchie standing on the porch with a few of his friends. He was staring at her, and she looked at Lucien.

"Hold on. I can't just leave without talking to Ritchie."

Lucien growled out, and she stopped, surprised the noise had come from him because it sounded enraged, animalistic even. "Let's just go, Callie," he said, but he was staring at where Ritchie stood.

"Lucien, stop it."

He snapped his gaze to her, and she felt her eyebrows pull down as confusion settled in her.

"What is wrong with you?" Callie asked.

He clenched his teeth, hardened his jaw, and looked as though he couldn't control himself. She wanted to believe that he cared about her so much his need to keep her close was strong, but she knew better. This was probably him looking out for his biker brother's daughter, feeling some kind of extra loyalty to Kink and her because of the kiss they had shared. He was feeling guilt, and being here, driving several hours out to come make sure she was okay, was proof of that. It was depressing to think of that way, but it was reality. Yes, he'd said he cared about her. Without saying anything else, or him responding to her question, she turned and walked toward Ritchie.

He was staring at Lucien a little nervously, and she felt horrible that he even felt like that. She climbed the few steps up to the porch, and the two guys that stood behind Ritchie looked away as she smiled. "Listen, I'm really sorry about just having to leave, but I think heading out is probably best."

She wasn't going to get into it that Lucien wouldn't think twice about throwing her over his shoulder if he thought it was best for her, or if his alpha caveman tendencies got the better of him. She also wasn't going to get into it that Lucien was a dangerous, hardened man, and compared to all these frat guys he'd crush them as if they were annoying gnats. Whatever was going on with Lucien, why he had honestly come up here as if on a whim, told her he might be even more unstable than normal. But what she wasn't going to tell Ritchie, or anyone for that matter, was that the outlaw biker that she felt still staring at her, was the man she loved more than she should, and that wanting him could cost her a lot.

"That guy is pretty damn scary, Callie," Ritchie said and chuckled a little nervously. "He's staring at me like he wants to wash his Harley with my blood."

Now it was her turn to chuckle, but hers also came out a little awkwardly, because Lucien was capable of such violence. "Yeah, he can be intimidating, but I think leaving now is probably for the best." She looked at Lucien, saw he was watching them like a predator waiting to pounce, and then turned her focus away from him. "He's my dad's friend, and liable to tell him I'm partying and hanging with a bunch of degenerates." She smiled, hoping to ease this weird tension between them.

"Hope you don't get in trouble over coming and hanging out with us, and I assure you we are not degenerates." He smiled, and it was genuine, and eased some of the strain.

She chuckled. "Everything will be fine. Lucien can just be—"

"Intense?" Ritchie said and cocked an eyebrow.

She smiled. "Something like that. Well, I'll see you later?" She phrased it like a question, because she honestly didn't know if him hanging out with a girl that had big ass scary bikers showing up to frat parties was something he wanted to be associated with.

He leaned against the banister and shook his head. "I can't fault you for who you associate with. Hell, look at the jokers that follow me around." He teased as he pointed to the two guys behind him. They flipped him off, but they were also smiling. "If I don't see you before you leave tomorrow, we'll catch up in couple of weeks when school starts. We'll leave the hardcore biker at home, though." He started laughing, and she smiled.

"See you later." She turned and headed back to where Lucien leaned against his motorcycle. She didn't want anything more than a friendship with Ritchie, and after the awkward almost kiss he had given her, and the issue with Lucien going all mercenary she knew that things would work out. Ritchie seemed like a genuinely nice guy, and maybe that was what she needed in her life. But even as she thought that and stared at Lucien, she knew that what she wanted and what she needed in her life where two totally different things. The more dangerous, "wrong" desire was what was winning.

He was now standing by his bike, his arms crossed, a scowl on his face, and looking every bit as badass as his reputation implied. She stopped in front of him, stared into his silver eyes and waited for him to say something … anything.

"Get on."

Callie moved to the back of the bike, keeping her mouth shut because she just wanted to have this night over with, and went to straddle the massive Harley. But before she could get on it Lucien had his hands around her waist, and was lifting her as easily as if she weighed nothing. Bracing her hands on the leather seat in front of her, she stared at him with what she knew were wide eyes.

"Here." He handed her the skullcap helmet, and once she had it on, he straddled the bike. For a second she was a little taken aback at being this close to him on his bike. Yeah, they had kissed, but for some reason this felt very intimate. His body heat seeped into her. Callie's thighs were on either side of him, holding him close, and her pussy growing wet from the closeness of being here with him. The big logo patch of The Brothers of Menace was etched into his cut, and she stared at that worn leather vest with the slightly dirty patch, which showed a phoenix and motorcycle.

"Unless you want to fall off the back of the bike you need to hold on, Callie," he said gruffly, but didn't turn around.

Looking at his lean waist and swallowing, she reached around and wrapped her arms around him. She shouldn't be feeling this nervous around Lucien, especially after what they had done this morning, but maybe that was why she felt this way? And before she knew what he was doing he grabbed her hip and pulled her forward. Her pussy came in contact with him. The scent of leather, cologne, and oil filled her nose, and the feeling of him hard and tense underneath her hands consumed her. She closed her eyes, trying to focus on anything but touching him, and failing miserably. He had his hand on both of hers, had them pressed to the small cold buckle of his leather belt, and she breathed in roughly. God, she needed to keep it together, and once she was in her room she could break down, because right now she was on the edge and toeing the line.

Chapter Seven

Callie stepped into her dorm, glanced over her shoulder and saw Lucien standing by the door. "I think I got it from here." She tried to sound stronger, but having him right behind her, looking at her like he could see right into her soul, was unnerving in the best of ways. She wanted to still be angry with him for just showing up and acting like her father, telling her what she should and shouldn't do, or who she should talk with, yet she couldn't help but remember the fact he had said he cared about her.

The ride to her dorm had only been a ten minute trip, but for those few moments she had held onto Lucien tightly. She thought about a life where nothing stood in their way and they could be together, and for just a second she envisioned that they were a couple. Despite their age difference, the fact that the club was his life and that being with her would destroy what he had, she could see herself loving this man with no obstacles in the way. He didn't move, didn't even respond to what she had said, so she opened her door and put him out of her mind. If he wanted to play the "I'm not going to speak, just stare hard at you" card, then she could do the same.

She tossed her purse on the bed, and when she turned around it was to see that he had come into her room and shut the door behind him. He didn't have his arms crossed over his wide chest anymore, but he still looked just as frightening and intense staring at her.

"You never answered why you're here, Lucien, and don't give me that crap that you wanted to check up on me because you were worried. *You* pushed me away, told me this wouldn't work out because of my dad, the age gap, and the club." She was feeling her emotions come to the surface, and she was not going to let that happen. "I agree that I don't want you and my dad to be on the outs because of something we may or may not do, but I can't have you showing up out of the blue and stirring things up."

She needed to stay level, because he was calm, collected, and standing there like nothing ever affected him. The only time she had seen his exterior resistance crack was when they had kissed back at the clubhouse just this very morning. He had opened up to her, showed her that there was this passion inside of him, this need and want, and it matched her own. But then he had pushed her away, and that brick wall of composure had gone back in place. He had been the cold biker President she had known all her life.

Right now he had the same expression, and it pissed her off, but broke her heart, too. She looked away, trying to compose herself. It was hard trying to push her feelings down, and if he really wanted her to move on him showing up like this was defeating that purpose. With her back still to him she spoke again, trying not to let her emotions show, but failing.

"You were able to avoid me for the last three months, and after one kiss and pushing me away I thought that was the end of it." She inhaled and then exhaled roughly. "You're making this harder," she whispered. She took one more steadying breath, and then turned to face him. A gasp left her at the fact Lucien was directly behind her.

He stared into her eyes for a suspended moment, and then grabbed her behind the head, pulled her forward, and claimed her mouth with his. She felt his muscles against her softness and moaned against his mouth. He stroked her lips with his tongue, and she opened for him instantly, accepting him completely, and not worrying about the consequences of what they were doing. She had her hands on his biceps, clenched and unclenched his bulging muscles, and moaned into his mouth. She became a fiend for him, and any and all thoughts that had to do with staying away vanished.

He stared at her for a second, not speaking, but searching her face with his gaze. She felt on display for this man, and knew that what he was about to say would change the way things had gone for the last three months.

"I want you, you want me, and I am going to claim you, Callie," he said against her mouth. "I am going to have every part of you until you know irrevocably that you are mine." He leaned back an inch, still had his hand behind her head and his fingers tangled in her hair, and breathed against her mouth. "Damn the consequences." He kissed her again and again, and she melted into him, loved that he held her so tightly, so thoroughly, and that she felt like they were one. "I have tried to fight how I feel for you, tried to stay away, and I was damn good at it for the last few months." He rested his forehead against hers, and she was stunned to see this man looking so vulnerable.

He wasn't the feared MC President that she had always known, but this man opening up to her and telling her how he felt. It may only happen this one time, but she wanted him, wanted all of him, and she didn't want to say something that would ruin this moment.

"I've been thinking about this moment for a long time, Lucien." She leaned up and kissed him, stroked her tongue along his mouth, and actually felt his body harden beneath hers, and then he trembled slightly. Right now there wasn't anything on this planet except the two of them.

"Callie," he groaned out, and grabbed a chunk of her hair to pull her head back gently. He kissed and sucked at her throat, ran his tongue up the length of her neck, and then stopped at her pulse point. She grew wet, so damn needy, and wanted to take this to the next level. Damn the consequences, like he had put it.

He was breathing heavily, and when he pushed his erection against her belly, a fresh gush of moisture left her. He was so big and so hard for her. She had never been this wet for a man, never had a man inflame her like he was. Yes, Callie was a virgin, and yes, right now she wanted Lucien to be the man that took that from her.

"We're alone, Lucien," she said breathlessly, and when he pulled back she knew she had to have this drugged-out look on her face. She felt drunk from his touch and kisses, and wanted to be so far gone with the feel and taste of him that she didn't think she'd survive. Lucien started kissing her again, grinding his massive erection against her belly like he couldn't get enough, and Callie was more than willing to be the outlet for his need.

"What I want is you, and that's going against everything I believe in with my brothers," he said in this pained voice. But then he held her face in his hands, tilted her head to the side, and stroked her lips with his tongue. "But like I said before, I want you, you want me, and I'm going to have you because the alternative is too damn hard."

"Can we just focus on you and me?" She let her head fall back on her neck slightly, closed her eyes, and loved when he started stroking her skin with his thumbs. "I just want you to be with me right now."

This growl of need left him. He stared down at her for a few seconds, almost like he was struggling with himself on what he should do, and then he was tearing her clothes away like an animal in heat. There she stood, in her bra and panties, her body starting to sweat from her arousal, and her need for him bursting through her. Despite the chill in the air she was overheated. Her nipples were hard, and she knew they were poking through the thin material of her bra. Her panties were soaked from her desire, and her clit felt swollen. If he touched her between her legs she'd surely come right then and there. She may be inexperienced in actually having sex, but she wasn't a prude, and had done enough with the couple of boyfriends she had been with that she knew what a guy liked.

The moonlight speared through the curtains, and when she reached out and flattened her hands on his cut, smoothed them down his chest, and stopped at the button and fly of his jeans, her fingers started to shake uncontrollably. She was scared and nervous, and her strength was leaving as the thought of being with Lucien in this very real way filled her. He took hold of her hands and brought them up to his mouth. There he kissed each of her fingers softly while watching her.

"Lucien." She breathed out his name, feeling her hands tremble even harder now. "I've never…" She trailed off, feeling a little embarrassed at her inexperience. She wanted to give him everything he needed as a man, wanted to be able to pleasure him as much as he would surely pleasure her.

"Oh Callie, baby." He pulled her close, cupped her cheek, and stared into her face. Even in the darkness she saw his nostrils flare and this possessive, dangerous look cover his face. "You're a virgin?" he almost groaned out.

He asked the question, and she nodded. But it was due to the way he said it, soft and low, and filled with a lot of emotion, that she felt her throat close. Lucien backed her up until the edge of the bed came in contact with the back of her knees. She slowly lowered herself to the bed, and stared up at him. He held onto her chin, tilted her head back, and braced his other hand on the bed as he leaned in close to her face. They breathed the same air for a second, and then he was kissing her again.

"Callie, baby. You're killing me here," he said against her mouth, and then groaned out loud. "I'm your first, and I'll be your fucking last," he said possessively, fiercely, and she knew without a doubt he was telling the truth. "Your cherry is *mine*." He stroked her lips with his tongue, and moved his hand down her chest, over her belly, and rested it on her panties. "Your pussy is *mine*." He pulled at her bottom lip with his teeth until she groaned out, and he slipped his hand inside the waistband of her underwear, but didn't so much as rub her clit. "*You* are mine."

She felt that truth deep in her body, and knew without a doubt he meant every word. He took a few steps back, started removing his cut, and then went for his t-shirt. When he was shirtless, and started working at undoing his belt, button, and zipper, she stared at his chest. Hard planes of muscle covered every inch of his broad chest. The large tattoo in the center of his chest was of the Brother of Menace logo. It beckoned her with the temptation of the dark side, the forbidden corner of her life that she had never thought she'd venture to. His arms were covered in ink, all dark and intricate as they told a story. Because she couldn't help herself, Callie let her eyes travel lower. A line of dark hair started below his navel and made a trail down his rippling abdomen to disappear beneath his pants. The low throb that had been present between her thighs now became a fierce pounding that demanded to be noticed.

"If only you knew what I see when I look at you." His voice was low and filled with heat. Finished getting undressed, he now stood there completely naked, unashamed or bashful of his nudity, and rock hard for her. "If only you knew that I'd kill anyone that hurt you." His words were low and deep and held a hell of a lot of threat.

Although this was what she wanted with every part of her being, could she actually surrender to her wants and give herself to Lucien? The thick erection he sported had her clenching her thighs together as need overtook her. Callie didn't say anything, couldn't even form words at that moment. She stood, her knees shaking, her legs threatening to give out on her, and took a step closer. They stood toe-to-toe now, the largeness of his body blocking out everything behind him. The force of his breathing brushed across her face, ruffling the tendrils of her hair in a soft caress. His chest rose and fell quick and hard, and the pulse at the base of his throat beat wildly. Was her need just as evident as his?

Her hands shook, but she lifted them and placed them on his hard, rippled abdomen. The hard muscles clenched under her palm, and she slid her hands up the rolling, defined hills of his chest, along his tattoo until she was tracing the lines of that ink with her fingers, and then rested her hands on each of his pecs. The beat of his heart was strong and steady, so unlike her rapidly pounding one.

"*Callie*." He said her name on a whisper.

If she derailed from what she wanted to do she wouldn't be able to regain her strength and continue with this. "No one will bother us. Meredith will be gone for the night, and the dorm is pretty much empty as everyone is out partying." She leaned into him, felt the heat from his body seep into hers, and closed her eyes. It felt good to feel his warmth with nothing between them. When she looked into his face, the fierce expression of desire reflected back at her increased her pulse and lust for him. Here she was, in nothing but her undergarments, with Lucien Silver naked and wanting her right before her.

Very gently she curled her fingers into the hard, yet pliant flesh at his chest.

"Be my first, Lucien."

He took her hand, held it on his chest, right over his heart, and said in a low voice, "I'll be your first, and your only, Callie. You're mine, and there isn't anyone or anything that will stop me from having you."

She swallowed and nodded. "But my dad."

He closed his eyes for a second, and although she shouldn't have said anything, that fact was a big deterrent in all of this.

"Can we not talk about your old man when I'm about to finally be with you?" He offered her a smile, and it changed his whole expression. "But I'll cross that bridge, and that war, when the time comes okay?"

She nodded, reached behind her to undo her bra, and let it flutter to the floor. Callie was about to be with Lucien, and she knew this would change everything.

Chapter Eight

Lucien stared down at Callie, took in the sight of her creamy, flawless flesh, of the way she was nice and plump in all the right places, and of how her breasts would overflow in his hands. She had been a tiny thing while growing up, and then it seemed like within one summer she'd blossomed into the woman that was standing before him right now. He was hard, harder than he had ever fucking been in his entire life, and although he should be backing away and not touching her, he couldn't stop himself. She was his drug of choice, his addiction, and he wanted to get lost in this, get lost *in* her.

He reached out and cupped one large breast. The weight was substantial, and his cock jerked forward. His balls drew up tight, and his muscles tensed. The image of spreading her out on this small-ass bed, opening her thighs so he could see her sweet, wet virgin cunt, and then shoving his dick into her, slammed into his head like a violent beast. He smoothed his other hand on her breasts, cupped both mounds now, and felt her nipples harden further under his palm. He should have never come up here, should have stayed away from her like he had done successfully for the last three months.

But the thing was, when he had heard Kink talk about her going to some party, all these fucked-up images of her being taken advantage had consumed him. So now here he was, touching a woman that was way too fucking young for him, yet who he was infatuated with. He wanted her like he had never wanted another woman, and craved her like he was starving and she was the only thing that could sate his hunger. He fucking loved her.

Being with her was so wrong, or at least he kept telling himself that, and maybe it was because of that fact that he wanted her like he did. But he knew that was a damn lie. He had never been in love, never wanted a woman for more than a few hours at a time in all of his forty fucking years of being on this planet. Yet with Callie he wanted to protect her because she was his, because he looked at her and knew that he'd kill for her, maim to keep her safe, and claim her in a way that was unstoppable and unbreakable. When he looked into her soft, sweet face, took in her long raven colored hair and bright blue eyes, he knew that what he felt for this woman had to be that elusive emotion … love.

He loved her, would do anything for her, even risk his relationship with his club and Kink.

She rested her forehead on his chest, and he closed his eyes just enjoying the feeling of having her this close. Wrapping his arms around her, he held her tightly and rested his chin on the crown of her head. He had sex with women that were whores on the best of days, that didn't care about men using their bodies. They liked it that way in fact, and he hadn't thought twice about it. But Callie was untouched, and her being a virgin meant he couldn't be rough and insatiable with her in bed—the way he liked his sex—at least not this time. They'd have to approach the Kink situation sooner rather than later, because he wanted her and wasn't going to give her up, no matter what.

He inhaled deeply, took in the light floral scent of her hair, and closed his eyes. He was used to taking what he wanted when he wanted it, but he'd be gentle with her, show her that she meant more to him than just a quick fuck. No matter how wrong this seemed, or what others would think, she meant everything to him.

She pulled back and looked up at him, and he cupped the side of her face. He leaned down and kissed her soft and slow. With her hands still on his chest he felt her smooth them down his abdomen until she wrapped her fingers around his erection. He groaned at the fact it was Callie that was touching him, gently stroking him. It made it that much more pleasurable. Moving his hand behind her head, he cupped her, held her as he deepened the kiss, and moved his tongue faster and harder against hers. His mind and body screamed for more, to be rougher, harder, but he fought those urges because right now he needed to show her that he could be a gentler man when it came to her.

When she moaned against him he moved his hands to cup her panty covered ass, squeezed the globes, and then lifted her easily. She wrapped her legs around his waist right away, ground her pussy on his cock, and he grunted from the contact. The hard length of his dick prodded between her legs, and he wished the material that separated her from his were gone.

With their mouths still fused, and her legs wrapped around him firmly, he started to move them toward the small bed again. He laid her on the bed. "Take off the panties, baby."

She breathed in and out fast, her breasts rising and falling from the force. She slipped her underwear off, and let them fall to the floor. The thatch of trimmed black hair that covered the top of her mound beckoned him, but the sight of her bare pussy lips had pre-cum slipping from the tip of his cock. The way her legs were wide open, giving him that prime shot of her wet, swollen, and red pussy, made him feel feral. He grabbed his shaft, started stroking himself from root to tip as he stared at her luscious body, and groaned out.

She sat up, reached for him, and pushed his hand away. He didn't know what she was doing until she was the one who started moving her hand up and down his dick, grabbed his balls with her other hand, and made him on the verge of coming.

But when she leaned forward and wrapped her lips around the crown of his shaft, he about came right in her mouth. She sucked on his cockhead, stroked the root of his erection, and he speared his hand in her hair. Lucien thrust back and forth gently at first, but the way she hollowed out her cheeks, sucked him in good and deep, had Lucien nearly losing it. He pushed her back on the bed until she was lying on it, her legs spread, and her lips parted as she breathed in and out harshly from her arousal.

She rested against the mattress and watched him. Lucien lifted his hands and smoothed them down her legs. The sound of her swallowing filled the too quiet room. For a suspended moment he did nothing but stare at where his hands rested on her inner thighs. A tightening started at the base of his spine the longer he stared at her pussy, and he needed to be buried inside of her tight, hot heat.

Be gentle. Go slow. Take your time.

"Please," she whispered into the darkness. "I need you, Lucien." She closed her eyes and let her head fall back when he moved his fingers along her silky folds.

He needed to make this good for her. "Look at me when I'm touching you, baby." His voice was soft, but there was a distinct note of command laced in the words, and he couldn't stop that from coming forth. He was hardened naturally from the life he led, but he was trying to be the man she deserved for this first time.

For several long seconds he didn't speak, just stared at her and continued to keep a firm, yet gentle hold on her inner thighs. Slowly he removed his hands from her. Sliding his hands up her body, he stopped right below her breasts. Lucien could feel how fast and hard her heart was beating. Moving onto his knees between her legs, he leaned forward and ran his tongue along her cleft. She tasted sweet and slightly musky, was soft beneath his lips, and he felt this string in him draw tight before snapping in half. He started licking and sucking at her, wrapped his lips around her clit until she was pulling at his hair and moaning out. She moved her hips back and forth, thrust her pussy firmly against his mouth, and then he felt her explode around him.

"*Please*," she whispered into the darkness. "I need to feel you inside of me." She stared at him.

"You're so fucking beautiful, Callie," Lucien whispered. "You're mine, baby. No one will have you but me." Although being gentle with her was coming more naturally than it ever had in his life, Lucien had to rein in his desire to thrust right into her. He caressed her in gentle sweeps of his fingers, mouth, and tongue, until goosebumps formed along her skin. "Every part of you is mine." He moved his hands up so they rested right under her breasts. "Look at me." He waited until she obeyed, and then he caressed her breasts, stroked her nipples, and loved that she arched into his touch.

He leaned up and took her mouth again, and Lucien became lost in the sensations of their lips, tongues, and hands moving along each other's bodies. She ran the pads of her fingers across his bare chest, and he shook slightly from the gentle contact. No woman had ever made him feel like that, feel like if he didn't have her he'd lose his fucking mind. But it wasn't just about sex. It was about claiming Callie as his own.

"Tell me this is right, that you want this, too," she said, as if she was delirious and trying to prove that what they were doing was right.

He gripped her chin in a soft hold, waited until she stared into his eyes, and then he spoke. "This, right here, you and me, is what is right. It feels good because you are meant to be mine. Only the best things in life are worth fighting for, and if they weren't worth the battle then they aren't worth the time it takes to ensure they are yours." He stared into her face. "*You* are worth fighting for, and I know I am going to have one hell of a war when it comes to making sure you stay mine."

She swallowed, and this small smile flitted across her lips.

"Now, just say you'll be mine no matter what." He was acting so out of character, but nothing had ever felt this good.

"I'm yours, Lucien."

And then he kissed her hard and possessively, and was about to take Callie in a way he had never taken a woman before.

****

His big body rested against Callie's, pressing her into the mattress and sending a lovely, heavy sensation coursing through her.

"I want you so much, baby," Lucien murmured against her throat, and she loved how his stubble scraped along her skin. He was so muscular, so big and heavy that she felt her breath leaving her. It was a pleasurable sensation. Warm, hard male flesh molded into hers, making the sweet anticipation of release just a reach away. His cock was long and big, and of course she was nervous about the pain that she would feel once he was inside of her.

Lucien's narrow hips fit perfectly in the cradle of hers, and the hard, impossibly thick length of him parted her labia. He moved his hips back and forth, rubbed her slickness along her pussy, coated his shaft, and had her so ready for him she was about to scream. She was wet, unbelievably so. A guttural groan left him, and he jerked his hips forward.

"It feels so good, Callie baby." He curled his fingers around her upper arms and pressed his hips into hers again, but harder this time. Over and over he did this, his length sliding up and down her cleft as he rocked against her. The tip of his erection bumped her clit on every upstroke, and Callie had to bite her lip or she would have begged for him to move harder, faster. She rose up slightly and stared down the length of her body. She saw his cock moving between her folds, watched the tip of his shaft rubbing her clit, and saw the pre-cum spilling out of him.

"I've wanted you from the moment I picked you up three months ago, baby." He rocked against her faster now. "My need for you is undeniable, and I don't want to fight it any longer." He was dry humping her, and bringing her closer to an orgasm. Another bump to her clit and she squeezed her eyes shut. So, so close to feeling that explosion. She fell back on the bed and breathed out as the sensations moved through her.

"I've wanted you for a long time, Lucien," she whispered into his hair. He still had his mouth at her throat, was still kissing and sucking at her skin, and she loved that he was erotically abusing her flesh.

He pushed up from her, one forearm braced on either side of her head, and looked down at her body. The dark slashes of his eyebrows were knitted in thought. The muscles in his jaw jumped beneath his stubble covered flesh.

"I don't want to hurt you, but—"

"Don't think about it. If I didn't want to be with you I wouldn't be here right now, Lucien." She reached up and touched the side of his face. Callie pushed herself up on her elbows and kissed the underside of his jaw. He groaned, and she heard him inhale deeply. When she lay back down, she took Lucien's hand and placed it between her breasts. He braced himself on his other arm and stared down at his hand. She then pulled his hand lowered until he was cupping her pussy. "I'm so wet for you."

He swallowed, and she watched the way his throat worked from the act. "Yeah, baby, you are really fucking primed for me," he whispered. He rubbed her clit softly for few seconds, back and forth until awareness traveled through her, starting between her legs and working its way up her body. Her nipples tightened as blood rushed to them.

He latched his lips onto her neck again, licked and sucked at her skin until it felt abraded in a good way. "You're so responsive." He ran his tongue up her throat. A moan left her, and he breathed out. Her senses were attuned to the little touches of his fingers on her body, to the scrape of his teeth on her collarbone, and to the rubbing motion of his hand between her thighs. He lowered his head, trailing wet kisses along the top of her breasts before finally latching his mouth on an aching, hard nipple.

God, so good. The wet sounds of his lips around her turgid flesh filled the room. Lucien's harsh, guttural groans filled her ears. Without thinking, Callie grabbed Lucien behind the back of the neck and brought his mouth to hers. She swiped her tongue along his lips, loving the harsh sound that came from him. The musky, sweet flavor of her was still on him, and she grew wetter from it. For several moments Lucien gave in and allowed her to explore his mouth.

"I need to be with you without anything, baby. I'm clean, always used protection, but with you I want to feel all of you."

She was on the pill to regulate her period, and although she shouldn't be stupid about this and insist he use a condom, she trusted Lucien with her life. "I trust you. I want to be with you, *all* of you."

Lucien looked down at her, and lifted his hand to run his thumb along the swell of her bottom lip.

"No more waiting, Callie."

She opened her mouth and sucked his finger between her lips. He moved his other hand between their bodies, bracing his weight on his elbows, and placed the tip of his dick at her entrance. She was so nervous, but she knew she wanted to do this more than anything else. A shock of pain went through her when he started to push his dick into her body, but she closed her eyes and held onto his biceps.

"So good. You're doing so good." He kissed the top of her head and continued to push into her.

The stretching and burning sensation was intense, but when he was fully inside of her she sighed. The feeling of being completely filled by the man she loved was breathtaking, and then when he cupped both sides of her face and kissed possessively, her pussy clenched around him.

"Callie…" Lucien said softly, but harshly, and started moving back and forth in her, slow and easy at first. The broad head of his dick stretched her unused muscles when he got to the entrance of her body, and then he pushed into her again. He did this over and over again until she was sweating with pressure and pleasure. With every inch he sank into her, Callie felt filled, claimed.

"So good, Callie baby."

Oh God.

He leaned back slightly and watched himself push into her and pull back out. She rose up on her elbows, saw the massive, long, thick length of him pull out of her, and her eyes widened at the sight of her blood covering his cock. It wasn't a lot, just a few streaks of red, but it was as if that sight meant something a hell of a lot more serious.

"It *is* fucking serious, Callie." Lucien said, and she realized she must have spoken out loud. "It means that you're mine, that this sweet fucking virgin pussy will only ever be mine. I claimed you, took your cherry, and because of that I can't let you go." He growled out the words, and thrust back into her. The play of muscles that rippled along his shoulders and biceps spoke of his strength, and a gush of moisture slipped from her, further aiding in his penetration. He pulled out slowly and pushed back in. Over and over he did this, slow and easy thrusts that had her lifting her hips in hopes he'd go faster. Beads of sweat dotted his brow and slid down his temple. The force it took for him to control himself was astounding, but she didn't want gentle, even though this was her first time. She wanted his sweat to drip on her as he pounded into her body. She wanted to just … *feel* Lucien Silver.

"I know you're holding back, and I don't want that, Lucien." Something shifted behind his eyes after she spoke, and his movements picked up, as if he couldn't control himself. His cock slid in and out of her, growing faster and faster as his hips slapped against hers and the sound of wet flesh filled the room.

"*Christ*, Callie," Lucien said harshly. He pushed himself up, leaning back on his haunches, and gripped her inner thighs. He pushed her legs impossibly wider and stared down at where his cock sank into her pussy. When he lifted his gaze back to hers he said hoarsely, "Look. Watch as I take you."

The pleasure was insurmountable, but when she braced herself on her elbows and stared down at where their bodies met once again, the ecstasy rose. He pulled his cock almost all the way out, and the glossiness from her cream and her virgin blood shone under the moonlight that came through the window. He placed his thumb on her clit and moved the bundle of nerves back and forth, over and over, and then she exploded without any preamble.

Lights flashed before her eyes as her orgasm claimed her. But Lucien didn't relent as he pistoned in and out of her, drawing her climax to the peak then keeping it there until she couldn't breathe. When the world came back into focus the image before her had her arousal racing to the forefront again. He looked wild, untamed, and full of heat. Sweat dripped down his chest in droplets and landed on her breasts. His short hair was wet from his perspiration, but he had never looked so good to her. Before she could even blink, Lucien moved onto his back and had her straddling him. His hands were on her waist, and he lifted her, forcing his cock to almost slip out before he impaled her on him again. Callie's head spun as he did this continuously. All she could do was brace herself with her hands on his chest as he fucked her on his shaft.

Grunts and groans left him and grew louder and louder. She knew he was close. Taking matters into her own hands, Callie pressed all the way down on him and ground her pussy on his pelvis. She was sensitive, sore even, but she wasn't going to stop this. A gasp left her when her clit rubbed against the short, coarse hairs of his lower belly.

"Yeah, Callie. Fuck, *baby*." He tightened his hold on her waist as she took over the rocking motions. Up and down she moved, sinking harder and faster on his cock until her head grew dizzy from it all. She was going to come again.

The taste of sweet release was so close that on the next down stroke she ground her clit against him. The explosion inside of her rivaled the one before. Callie threw her head back and cried out as her pussy clamped down on his cock. Lucien dug his fingertips into her, and his low, animalistic grunt signaled he'd found his own release. If it were even possible, she felt him harden even further inside of her.

She collapsed against his chest, their skin sweaty and their breathing cacophonous. He wrapped his arms around her and rolled so they were on their sides facing each other. The heavy length of him was still buried inside of her, and spasms continued to travel through her. Closing her eyes and resting her forehead on his damp chest, she listened to the sound of his heart beating.

After several minutes of silence, and the feel of Lucien stroking his fingers up and down her back, she pushed back and braced herself on an elbow, staring down at him. For a second he just stared at her, and then lifted his hand to cup her cheek.

"What is it, baby?" he said softly.

"Nothing." She smiled. "Well, that's not true. I'm just worried about how all of this will play out with my dad and the club when all of this comes to light." She lay on her side and stared at the ceiling. The bed was small, barely big enough to hold her, but having Lucien's massive body on it, too, required her to be pressed right up against him, nearly lying on top of him. "Because I don't want this to be the only time we see each other." She looked over at him. He was staring at the ceiling, his jaw locked tight as he looked deep in thought. She had contemplated not saying anything, not wanting to ruin this moment, but it needed to be said, because that was their reality. "I love you, Lucien," she said softly, and when he looked at her Callie's heart jumped in her throat.

"Everything will work out, Callie, because I'll make sure it does." He kissed her on the forehead again, and she loved this gentleness in him. "Because I've never loved anyone the way I love you, and I meant it when I said I wouldn't let anyone or anything take you away from me."

Chapter Nine

Lucien grabbed a tool from beside him and started taking apart the engine in the rusted out Harley. He had been in the garage at the clubhouse for the last three hours, and mainly it was to keep his mind off Callie. It had been two long fucking weeks since he had been with her, and to say that it was damn hard was an understatement. But she had been staying busy by packing up the rest of her things for school.

Did it suck that she'd be several hours away when they had just started being with each other? Yeah, it fucking sucked, but he wasn't going to hold her back by being a selfish bastard. She needed to go to college, to learn and make something huge out of herself, even if she had told him she didn't know what she wanted to do with her life. The point was she was out there taking the initiative, and that was what he wanted for her. She was a smart young woman—*his* woman—and he wouldn't tell her what she should and shouldn't do when it came to living her life. Now, those fuckers that she'd be going to school with, well, they better watch their damn manners, and keep their hands to themselves, because if they so much as looked at her wrong and he found out he'd beat their asses to the ground. Lucien never pretended to be something he wasn't. He had always been a violent man toward the ones that wronged him or the ones he considered his family. But with Callie he found himself even more possessive, dominant, and he didn't care if others saw how he acted toward her as being over the top alpha.

Being inside of her that one time hadn't quenched his need for her, and in fact made him want her more, made him feel like this possessive obsessed animal that couldn't stop until she was his. But she *was* Lucien's, and nothing would change that. He sure as fuck wasn't an insecure man, and knew what he wanted in all things, but he also felt a little unsure about where he was going with Callie because he'd never felt this way before. He ached for her, but not just to be with her sexually. He wanted to hold her, to kiss her. Hell, he'd even settle on going for a ride with her on his Harley and sitting there in silence. He just wanted *her*.

Talking on the phone to her in private, and making sure none of the other members heard them, made him feel like a sneaky fucking bastard. It wasn't like he didn't want to tell Kink that he loved Callie with this deep-rooted need that bordered on obsession. He needed to go about this the right way, because as it was he had fucked up big time by not telling Kink how he felt for Callie right away. It was more about the timing. He had been trying to decide how to go about this, but the last couple of weeks had opened his eyes to a lot of things: his feelings, what he wanted out of life, and what he wanted with Callie. This was a sensitive subject, and it wasn't like he was just going to come out and tell Kink that not only was he fucking his daughter, but that he was also madly in love with her. He wanted a life with Callie, wanted to have a family one day with her. She needed to have her own life, experience things, too, but he only wanted her. He might have never felt this way, or wanted an old lady, but she was his, he had claimed her, and nothing would change his mind on the end result.

They needed to tell Kink, and the other members, too, because this involved them as well. A club member didn't keep things from his brothers, but Lucien was doing just that and he felt like a piece of shit because of it.

His cell rang, and he grabbed a rag and cleaned his hands off before answering it. He saw the flash of

Callie's number on his screen, and he felt like a damn teenager for how happy he was when he saw that it was her. Lucien stood and glanced out the open bay doors of the garage. He made sure he was alone, and then he answered the phone.

"Hey, baby." He turned away from the clubhouse and went to his workbench.

"Hey yourself," she said softly.

He was getting hard just from hearing her voice. "You nearly packed?" She'd be heading off to the university next weekend—only a few days away—and only be coming back to River Run for holidays and on weekends, and that was going to be damn hard. But he didn't cancel out the fact he was probably going to show up randomly, just to make sure she was okay, and to tame the urge to touch her on a constant basis.

"I am, but I was thinking…" She paused, and he knew what she was going to say.

He turned and looked at the clubhouse, saw Kink leaving with a few of the other guys, and felt this gut-wrenching ache of betrayal. Lucien closed his eyes and exhaled roughly. He knew that he couldn't betray Kink anymore. "Baby—"

"Lucien, I can't do this behind my dad's back anymore. We have to tell him about us."

He breathed out, feeling this relief fill him, but it was short-lived when Kink stopped and waved at him.

"Later, brother. I'm heading home to be with my girls," Kink shouted out, and Lucien lifted his hand goodbye.

"Yeah, baby, we need to tell him now, because this is a bad situation already, and the longer we keep it from him the worse it'll get." He wasn't about to tell her that when they did tell Kink he would go bat-shit crazy, kick Lucien's ass, and worry about the damage afterwards.

"I know." She sighed, and he hated that she was feeling this way. "How about you come over tomorrow? We'll have dinner, and we can tell my dad together?" She sounded unsure, a little frightened, and he hated that she was feeling these turbulent emotions.

"Callie, everything will be okay. I'll make sure it is." He wanted to pull her close right now, to hold her, kiss her, and make sure she didn't feel like this. Yeah, he was totally fucking gone for this woman, and there was no changing the fact that it would only get more intense.

"I'll text you the time to come over, but I want this out of the way, Lucien. I don't want to have to talk to you behind anyone's back. I don't want to hide my relationship with you, and I hope you wouldn't either."

"No, baby. The last thing I want to do is keep how I feel for you in the dark. I've already done it for too long." She was breaking his fucking heart. Of course he didn't want to hide their relationship, and although they didn't have some childish title to go along with what was happening with them, she was his and that was more than any boyfriend or girlfriend label that someone came up with. He was old enough to know what he wanted in life, and that what he had with Callie was real. "Baby, I want to be able to hold you, kiss you, and have my way with you anytime and anywhere. I don't want to have to do anything behind someone's back, least of all a Menace brother."

"People will get hurt, Lucien. It's inevitable. And I don't want that, but I also love you and don't want to not be able to be with you because of what others think."

"I know, Callie baby, and we'll figure it out." He stayed on the phone with her for a few more minutes, and when they hung up he stared at the driveway. He was the worst kind of person to be doing what he was doing behind Kink's back, but tomorrow he'd rectify that, because the truth needed to come out, like three fucking months ago.

****

Callie was a nervous wreck, and it was because of two things. Tonight Lucien was coming over with a few of the guys from the club for dinner, and her dad had been the one to set it up. She hadn't even had time to ask her father about having Lucien over. Kink had been the one to arrange this, to invite some of the guys over that weren't on a run, because he said he had something to talk to them about. He had been distant, concerned even when he looked at her. She worried that he knew already about them, that maybe he had somehow heard from someone that she was with Lucien. Cookie even seemed a little off, like she was avoiding Callie, and that had her worried that maybe she should just come out and say everything before they had a room full of people. Why he would want some of the club members present when this was all said was beyond her. Although they were all like family, this was something that she'd hoped to just tell her dad at first.

Glancing at the clock she saw that it was a half past six in the evening. Lucien, Cain, and Tuck were supposed to be coming over to eat, and Cookie was still in the kitchen preparing things. Lord, she was a nervous mess. Not only had she hardly seen Lucien since she had been back in River Run, but they were going to lay it all out in the open, and let the chips fall where they did.

"You okay, Callie?" Cookie asked.

Callie turned away from the clock and stared at the other woman. "Yeah, I'm fine, just wondering what tonight is all about since my dad called some of the guys over." She rubbed her hands on her thighs. She had texted

Lucien earlier tonight, hoping he had some kind of insight on why Kink wanted them over tonight, but he had been as clueless as she was. Hell, Kink had been the one to sit her down and tell her that they needed to talk, that some of the guys were coming over, and that it was really important that she be there. She was afraid of what he was going to say, of how things would play out, but she had no choice in the matter and would just have to stick it out. If they weren't going to bring up the fact she was with Lucien, then she'd still have to bring it up tonight. This had gone on long enough, and she planned on talking about the last three months, her feelings, and how she was going to be with Lucien because she loved him.

"It'll be okay," Cookie said cryptically, and Callie watched as the other woman turned away and started busying herself in the kitchen. She was overly trying to distract herself, that was for sure, and Callie wondered exactly what in the hell was going on. Callie had never seen Cookie act like she was on edge or nervous, but tonight she was definitely showing those characteristics.

"Everything okay, Cookie?" The other woman might be only a few years older than Callie, but she looked at Cookie as a role model. After all the shit Cookie had been through in her life, and had still stayed strong and prevailed, she was someone that Callie wanted to take after, wanted to learn from, and seeing her nervous like this was a little unsettling. Cookie always seemed in control. Even when Callie had gotten the news about her mother passing away Cookie had been there, giving her the strength she needed not to totally break down.

Cookie turned around and nodded. "Of course, honey." Cookie had started using those motherly endearments after Callie's mom had passed away, and although at first it was a little strange hearing the slightly older woman calling her them, Callie couldn't lie and say it wasn't comforting. She liked hearing them, in fact.

"You sure? You look a little nervous, and it's kind of freaking me out. Well, even more than tonight already is."

Cookie nodded and then swallowed loudly. "I…" She glanced down, twisted the towel in her hands, and then looked back up at Callie again. "You should know before you're bombarded in there with all the guys."

"Okay…" Callie stared at her, feeling her entire body strung tight. "What's going on?" Her heart was racing, and she had a feeling this most definitely had to do with her and Lucien. Damn, had someone overheard them talking? She wouldn't put it past one of the guys to have followed Lucien up to the university just to see what he was up to, although that would have been shady behavior. But then again they would have seen what Lucien was doing as the same fucked up thing. "I don't like surprises, and this whole weird and funky vibe I am getting from you and Dad is making me feel like I'm walking on eggshells."

Cookie moved over to her, stared into her eyes, and for a moment all Callie could see on Cookie's face was pure uncertainty.

"Callie, your dad and I wanted to talk to you about something that we've just found out." Cookie swallowed roughly. "We have known for a while, and have wanted to talk to you about, but he was freaking out, and I didn't know what to say, and…"

"Oh God." Callie moved away, feeling her face heat, because she had known this was about Lucien and her. "We actually meant to tell you, Cookie." She turned around and faced the other woman. "We were going to tell you and my dad today, because we were tired of sneaking around, and it felt like this big betrayal."

Cookie didn't respond, but she knitted her eyebrows in confusion. "You were going to tell us tonight?" Cookie asked.

Callie nodded. "Yeah, I was going to cook dinner, and Lucien was going to come over, and we were going to tell you guys about it all, but it looks like you knew already." She rubbed her forehead and breathed out. "We just didn't know what to say, but you guys already know. What I don't understand is why you'd invite the other two guys along? I know the rest of the members are on a run, but I would have preferred if this stayed among the four of us. Not that I don't love the guys like my family, but, well, you know." She shrugged.

"Callie, sweetheart." Cookie took a step closer. "You were going to tell us about you and Lucien being together tonight?" Cookie sounded confused, and shocked.

Oh. Shit.

"You and Lucien? Like Lucien, the President of the club?" Cookie whispered the last part, her eyes wide.

The sound of the doorbell ringing stopped Callie from responding. But she wouldn't have known what in the hell to say anyway.

"Hey, can one of you get that?" Kink called out from the next room, and Callie stared at Cookie, and then looked at the front door.

"I'll get it," Callie said way too softly for anyone but Cookie to hear. She hadn't said anything to Callie, but she did continue to stare at her with this shocked expression on her face. "Yeah, I'll just go get that." She turned away and went to the door, her knees shaking, and her legs feeling like they'd give out at any second. When she grabbed the handle and turned it, pulled the door open, and took in the three massively huge bikers standing on the porch, she looked at Lucien immediately. There he stood, in front of the other two men that were talking softly with each other, and his silver eyes trained right on her.

"Callie." He said her name softly, and when the other two men, Cain and Tuck, pushed past him and came inside, they still stood there staring at each other.

Callie wanted to tell him that tonight wasn't about them, or at least it hadn't been. She still didn't know what her dad and Cookie were going to say, but now Callie worried that Cookie would tell everyone what Callie had said in the kitchen. But whatever Cookie and Kink were going to tell them was definitely important for them to call this impromptu dinner, and she thought that was a little unnerving on its own. She stepped aside to let Lucien in. This was the first time she had seen him since being back from her orientation. It was safer, and smarter, just to keep their distance until they could tell her dad about all of this. But it was damn hard, and when he walked by, purposefully brushing his hand along hers in passing, this thrill of electricity moved through her. He smelled good, masculine and potent, and reminding her of everything that was Lucien Silver. She stared at the way his jeans molded to his hard body, and at the fact his dark t-shirt and cut didn't hide the play of muscle underneath the material. She remembered vividly what he looked like with nothing on, so strong and big, towering over her as he thrust deep into her body and took her virginity.

"Brother." Her father's voice came through in a booming bass, and she moved away from Lucien to shut the door. The two men clapped each other on the back, and it was so strange to see the man she loved and her father embracing as if what she and Lucien were doing behind everyone's back wasn't their reality. Her dad seemed tense, though, and she wondered, if they weren't going to confront them, what was making them act so weird.

Chapter Ten

They all sat around the table, Tuck and Cain seeming oblivious to the fact that the rest of them were looking at each other with shifty eyes, wondering what in the hell was happening, but not speaking. They had finished eating about ten minutes ago, and the silence was starting to become thick and uncomfortable. Callie grabbed her water, took a sip, and looked at Lucien from over her rim. He sat between Cookie and Cain, and her dad was at the head of the table, his focus on the beer bottle in front of him.

"I called you here tonight because I have something that I need to tell everyone." Kink looked at everyone, and Cain and Tuck stopped eating their apple pie and glanced at him. "I figured we could have waited until all the guys were back from the run, but I wanted to tell everyone now since Callie will be heading back to college and you're all my family." He looked at Cookie. "Besides, we didn't want to wait."

"What's going on?" Callie shifted in her seat, and looked between Cookie and her dad. When she looked at Cookie again it was to see that she was staring right at her. Cookie had this worried, almost horror-filled expression on her face, and then she glanced at Lucien, as if wanting to say something, but fortunately not saying anything. When Callie looked at Lucien it was to see this blank expression on his face, his body relaxed in the chair, and one arm resting on the table. He looked calm, but Callie knew he was ready for anything.

"You want to tell them or should I, Cookie?" Kink said, and when Callie looked at her dad she saw, for the first time in her life, this vulnerable expression on his face. All eyes turned to Cookie, and then she smiled big.

"We didn't mean to worry anyone," Cookie said and looked pointedly at Callie. "But, we wanted to tell you all, well, the ones that are here at least, that we are having a baby."

The room was silent for a second, everyone staring at each other, and then Tuck and Cain burst out in joyous shouts.

"I'm about five weeks along, and this is totally a surprise to us," Cookie said and started wringing her hands together. And then she looked at Callie. "We didn't plan this, but we are happy about the news."

Cain and Tuck stood and walked over to Kink, who was now out of his seat. He had this goofy smile on his face, and clapped the other men on the back as they gave each other those manly hugs guys did with each other. Lucien stood and did the same thing with her dad, and they spoke softly, both hugging again. Callie stood, and her dad and Cookie were not looking at her, maybe thinking she'd freaking out.

"Sweetheart, we didn't plan this, and although the time isn't right—"

She shook her head, stopping her dad from finishing. Yeah, it was only a few months since her mom had passed away, but that didn't mean life stopped for the grieving process. She might not have had the best relationship with her mother, might have wished on a hundred different occasions that she could just leave because she was finished with living with her, dealing with her bullshit, and have to fight her on everything. But she was moving on, going forward with her life, and she wanted her dad and Cookie to do the same.

"I think it's the perfect time." Callie smiled and saw the relief on her dad's face. He came up to her and wrapped his arms around her, and gave Callie a big bear hug.

"I'm glad you're okay with this, sweetheart. I worried that maybe you'd be upset because this is pretty soon after your mom…"

She shook her head. "We need to all move on with our life, Dad. And although I miss Mom, and did love her, we can't worry about if it is too soon to do something." She pulled back and looked at her dad's face.

"You're pretty damn smart, baby girl." He leaned down and kissed her on the head, and she glanced at Lucien over her dad's shoulder. He watched them, this strange look on his face, but one that made her feel happy. Lucien made her feel special, wanted, and like nothing would ever hurt her.

"Come on, brothers, let's go drink and celebrate," Cain said, and the four men moved into the living room.

Cookie still sat at the table, and when Callie turned toward her she stood.

"Congratulations," Callie said and gave Cookie a hug.

"You're okay with being a big sister?" Cookie asked and chuckled softly.

"You ready to be a mom?" Callie asked and pulled back, smiling.

Cookie stared at her for a moment, and then grinned. "I think I really am." They pulled away from each other, and then she tilted her head toward the kitchen. Callie followed her father's old lady, and once they were several rooms away from where the men were, Cookie turned and faced her.

"Tell me everything, Callie, because this is serious shit."

Callie nodded and exhaled. "Yeah, I know." She stared at the woman that was like a best friend to her, that had been there during her hardest time, and that she looked up to. "But I love him, Cookie, and he loves me," she said softly, feeling all of her emotions rise up. "We didn't mean to do anything behind anyone's back, but it just kind of happened."

The sound of the guys laughing had Callie looking behind her into the hallway. Her heart was in her throat, and she was so nervous about saying all of this out loud.

"How long has this been going on exactly?" Cookie asked, and Callie looked back at her.

"Officially? Like two weeks but we've stayed away since I've been back from orientation. We planned on telling Dad, but the time was never right."

Cookie shook her head and leaned against the counter. They stared at each other for a suspended moment. "Tell me what in the hell happened."

For the next several minutes Callie told Cookie everything. She told her about the party and Lucien taking her back to his place because she didn't want her dad finding out. She told him how she had fallen madly in love with him, and how he had pushed her away for months until he had come to the university and they had finally been together.

"So … you were like with him?" Cookie was sounding more and more shocked with each passing second.

Callie didn't go into detail, but she did nod.

"Damn, Callie, this is so bad."

"No, Cookie, it's not bad in the sense that we love each other."

Cookie shook her head. "No, I'm not saying it's bad that you love him." She moved closer. "This is bad because you're with the President of the club, and hid it for three months from your dad and everyone else, Callie." Cookie took Callie's hands and gave them a light squeeze.

"We didn't hide anything for the last three months aside from the fact Lucien helped me out when I was at that party. Nothing happened at all until two weeks ago." Of course that wasn't an excuse. "I should have told my dad about the whole party and me being drunk and going to Lucien's the next day at the latest, but I was afraid of the repercussions within the club. I didn't want anyone to get upset with Lucien for keeping it from them." She shrugged, looked at the ground, and refused to cry. "But then everything just escalated when he was at the university with me. My feelings have only grown, even though he's tried to push me away and kept his distance."

"Oh, honey," Cookie said and pulled her into a hug. "Everything will be okay."

"No, no it won't be, Cookie." Callie shook her head. "My dad will feel betrayed, and I can see why he would, but I honest to God love Lucien."

Cookie pulled back and looked into her eyes. "And he loves you?" she asked, and Callie nodded.

"He does. I know he does by the way he looks at me, touches me, and speaks to me. He's different when he's around me, if you can believe that."

Cookie gave her this soft smile. "Yeah, honey, I know exactly what you mean."

****

It was late, Cookie had called it a night an hour ago, and Cain and Tuck had already headed back to the clubhouse to finish partying. Lucien was happy for Kink and Cookie, knew that the club was just as much a part of his family as his old lady and daughter were, but wished they could have come clean about each other. Tonight was obviously not the night to talk to Callie's dad about Lucien wanting her as his old lady, about how he loved her, would do anything for her and was so damn sorry for betraying Kink the way he had.

He grabbed his keys out of his pocket, and although he wanted to go and see Callie before he left, he knew that wasn't the wisest choice right now.

"Heading out, brother?" Kink said from the stairway, and Lucien turned and faced him.

"Yeah, it's getting late."

Kink nodded. He scrubbed a hand over his hair, looked back at the bedroom door Cookie had slipped behind, and then this smile broke out across his face. "Can you believe I'm going to have another kid?"

Lucien grinned. "Man, I hope you're prepared for that. You're getting pretty fucking old."

Kink started chuckling, and then flipped him off. "Yeah, I know. And if it's another girl I'm fucked, because I'm already freaking the fuck out about Callie going off to college and those motherfuckers messing with her."

Lucien cleared his throat, opened his mouth to just tell Kink about every fucked up and shady thing he had done and thought about concerning Callie, but then the object of his affection, obsession, and love walked through the kitchen door. She stopped, looked between them, and he could see how nervous she was. Hell, this right here was an awkward situation.

"Listen, I'm going to head to bed anyway, but I'll see you at the clubhouse tomorrow."

Lucien nodded. "Sounds good, brother." Lucien should have just left, but instead he stood by the front door and stared at the way Kink embraced Callie, kissed her on the top of the head, and then turned and headed toward his bedroom.

Callie stared at him, smiled softly, and he wanted to kiss her, hold her, and tell her that they didn't need to hide anymore. But today, now, was not the fucking time. "I'll see you later, Callie."

She swallowed, ran her hands on her thighs, and then nodded. "Bye, Lucien."

Damn, he was getting hard hearing her say his name. He wanted her so damn badly, and the fact it had been two weeks since he had touched her was eating away at him. Before he said something, or did something, that would disrespect Kink in his home, he turned and headed out of the front door and to his bike. He straddled his Harley, grabbed his helmet, but then he heard the front door open and close, and saw Callie moving toward him with her bare feet padding on the cement. Before he knew what she was doing she was in his arms, her mouth on his, and her tongue sweeping along his. Callie had her arms wrapped around his neck, and he grew hard for her. Fuck, he wanted her so damn badly.

"Baby, we can't do this. We can't disrespect Kink this way, not anymore."

She pulled away, breathing heavily, and her mouth glossy and red from their kiss. I know, but I missed you. I *miss* you, Lucien."

"Damn, Callie, I miss you, too," he said softly, and then grabbed the back of her head and kissed her soundly. He ran his tongue along hers, swallowed her moans, and knew that he should stop, but not able to end his obsession for her. Kink was right inside. Lucien wanted to respect his brother and VP, but he couldn't stop. He couldn't bring himself to pull away, to do the right thing.

"You're right," Callie said against his lips, and pulled away. They were both now breathing hard. "We need to tell him, but tonight isn't good, not when they broke the baby news." She looked down at the ground. "But tomorrow, since he'll be at the clubhouse, the guys are still on the run, and we can be open and honest."

He nodded. Taking hold of her chin with his fingers, he lifted her head so she looked at him. "Yeah, baby, tomorrow we will tell him, and then we won't have to hide. Everything will work out." But he knew that wasn't the truth, because shit was going to get real, and blood would be shed.

"Let's go for a ride, Lucien," She said softly, and then smiled. "My dad and Cookie went to bed, and believe me when I say they won't be coming out all night." She grimaced, and then shook her head in disgust. "Believe me."

He started chuckling. "Callie, that probably isn't the best idea right now."

"I know, but I just want to be free, to be on the back of your bike, and when we tell my dad I know being with you is going to be hard." She looked at the front door. "Just as hard as it is now, because he'll be furious, Lucien, and rightly so." She looked at him again. "Just let us enjoy this moment of solace in being together."

Looking at her face, taking in the small slope of her nose, the bow-like quality of her red lips, and the softness and brightness of her blue eyes, he knew he couldn't deny her anything, even when he should. When he didn't respond, but lifted the corner of his mouth in a smile, she leaned up and kissed him softly.

"Let me get my shoes." She looked sad almost, and he smoothed a finger down the bridge of her nose. "Just a quick ride, Lucien, because I know after this is all said and done things will definitely be different." She turned and went back into the house, and he exhaled. He was a piece of shit friend right now. He knew better than to keep this going on even though he knew it was wrong until they spoke with Kink. He was a bastard, but loving Callie meant he couldn't stay away, couldn't stop being with her, even though that was what a brother, a member of The Brothers of Menace, should do.

****

Callie tightened her hold on Lucien's waist and rested her cheek against his back. If there was an outsider looking in at all of this, what she and Lucien were doing and how they were keeping all of this from her dad, they would probably see her and Lucien as a bunch of betraying assholes. But that wasn't how she saw it. She saw it as not wanting to hurt her dad, as loving a man that others would consider to be forbidden, given who he was and who she was. But Callie couldn't help how she felt, and didn't want to stop her emotions, or be suffocated by what others considered wrong and traitorous.

Lucien held onto both of her hands with one of his, and gave them a light squeeze. She closed her eyes and listened to the rumble of his Harley beneath them, of the wind moving over their bodies, and of the scents invading her nose. His cut was smooth leather and buttery soft, and the smell of age and of it being well cared for filled her nose. The strength and power she felt from Lucien consumed her. It might have only been a short amount of time that she had actually *been* with Lucien, but they were the most alive and exhilarating two weeks of her life. After months of pining after him, wanting something she never thought she'd have, she was finally feeling whole. It was strange feeling this, having this solidity in her life, and feeling like things were finally right.

They had been riding for the last twenty minutes, were still near River Run, but were outside of the city. The trees surrounded them, and the moon was full and bright enough that she could see clearly. She didn't know what the future held, but she knew that she wouldn't give up on what she wanted, no matter what anyone said. And what she wanted was Lucien Silver, a man twice her age, the President of an outlaw biker gang, and her father's friend. She just hoped her dad saw that being with Lucien made her happy, and that he accepted it because this was her life.

Chapter Eleven

Kink was due at the clubhouse a little later that day, and although Lucien was relieved to finally be at this point where everything would be out in the open, he was also nervous over Kink's reaction. This was a man that had been there for him no matter what, that had risked his life for Lucien on more than one occasion, and who was like family to him. Kink was going to be hurt, and although Lucien wished things hadn't gone down this way, he also wouldn't take anything back he had done with Callie. Yes, he had pushed her away at first, and forced himself to focus on things that weren't forbidden to him, but obviously his feelings weren't just passing.

The sound of a door opening had him turning away from the paperwork he had been going over. Aside from a few prospects and Cain and Tuck, the rest of the members were on a run to seal down some land in The Springs, along with a crate full of guns in trade for coke. The Brothers didn't mess with drugs normally, but after getting a stash in trade for taking down some punks that were harassing local community college girls in Harlow, coke had been their payment.

There was the sound of footsteps coming closer, and he stood and moved toward the door. He saw Callie looking around the main club floor, and then she stopped and stared at him.

"Hey, what are you doing here so early?" he asked, knowing she wasn't supposed to be here for another hour, right before Kink showed up. He leaned against the doorframe and crossed his arms over his chest. She looked good, really damn good in fact. The denim skirt she wore wasn't obscenely low, but he saw a good amount of her lush thighs, and his cock jerked painfully behind his zipper.

She shrugged, and then smiled slowly. "I know, but I had to go to the store to pick up a few more things for my dorm…" She got silent, as if saying those things upset her.

"Hey, what's wrong?" He moved toward her, took her hand in his, and gave it a light squeeze.

"Is it bad that I wish I was staying in River Run with you?"

He knew what she meant, but was not about to let her ruin her life because of him. Lucien pulled her right into the meeting room and shut the door behind them. Stroking his hand over her hair, he stared into her bright blue eyes, and knew that this woman could be the end of him. She held his heart in her hand, and he didn't even think she knew it.

"Baby, I know what you mean, but no fucking way am I going to let you even entertain the idea that you're staying here because of me." He scanned her face with his gaze, took in everything that made her up, and felt his love for her grow to an even more dangerous level. "You are going to get that business degree, come back home to work with the club, and everything else will fall into place." She had told him that was what she wanted, and although saying it out loud to her, making her hear her own words, might upset her more, she needed to know he wanted this for her.

She shook her head, glanced down, and when she looked at him again she was smiling. "I could stay in River Run and go to the community college so that I'm close to you, Lucien."

He couldn't help but feel this warmth fill him, shit, *consume* him, at her words. "I love you, Callie Roberts. I love you so fucking much it makes me feel like a bastard for thinking I can actually have something good and right in my life." He continued to stare into her eyes, felt his cold, once dead heart start to beat hard and fast, and then leaned in to whisper against her mouth. "You're my fucking woman, Callie, my old lady, and I'd do anything for you." And then he shook his head. "But I won't let you ruin your life, your future. You'll go to Baker, become even smarter, and when you're done with school you'll make something incredible out of your life." He started moving his thumb along her cheek. "But I'll be here, baby. I'm not going anywhere, because you're mine, I'm yours, and that's how it's always going to be."

Callie nodded, and then her smile widened. "You're right, but not about ruining my life."

He let go of her, turned to face the small window in the meeting room, and stared at the few prospect that were working on bikes in the garage. They were alone, well, for the next hour at least, and although he shouldn't be thinking about anything aside from the upcoming conversation he'd have with Kink about his daughter, when he turned around all he wanted to do was kiss her. He stared at her, and the way she looked at him, a little nervously, had him moving closer.

Callie retreated a step. She might be trying to escape him, but she smiled, looked excited even, and he wasn't going to let her get away until he tasted her. Callie was eager for his touch, he could tell in the way her pulse beat at the base of her neck, and the way she was breathing harder, faster. She moved back another step.

"You running from me, baby?" His voice was low. He could tell she was aroused, that she wanted him, even though this was the most inappropriate time. When the wall stopped her retreat, and she placed her hands flat behind her, he moved closer until their chests nearly brushed together. He took a deep breath in, inhaling her scent, memorizing it.

"I'm not running."

He leaned in so their breaths mingled together and their mouths were only separated by an inch. "No?" He cocked a brow.

She shook her head, licked her lips, and said, "No. I'm not running." Her voice was soft and had a whisper-like quality even.

"Is that right, baby?"

She nodded and closed her eyes, exhaling a shaky breath out in the process. He dipped his gaze down to her lips. He took her mouth in a deep, penetrating kiss, fucking her like he had between her legs with his mouth and cock. Lucien was forceful with his actions, slamming his hands on the wall beside her head and pressing his cock into her belly. A hoarse groan left him when she stroked his tongue with her own. He broke away far too soon, and she blinked several times.

He slid his hands down the wall, touched her shoulders, stroked her arms, and took hold of her hands. "You're mine, Callie. I love you, baby."

It was like he was this mushy ass romantic man now. Being with her had changed something in him, and he fucking loved it. She was the one to slam her mouth on his now, and the soft moan that left her had his cock shooting forward, growing hard and uncomfortable with the need to be buried deep inside of her.

He slid his hands behind her to cup her ass, and in one effortless move he lifted her off her feet. She wrapped her legs around his waist and tilted her head to the side to deepen the kiss. Lucien was so fucking hard for her, loved that she was taking this initiative to be with him, to show him that she wanted him, too. He leaned back an inch, took in the way her skirt was hiked up her creamy, thick thighs, and he pressed his dick against her panty covered pussy. She moaned, let her head fall back against the wall, and he started kissing her throat. He thrust against her again, ground his cock on her cunt, and wanted to just pull her panties aside, get his dick out, and push right into her wet little body.

"That feels so good, Lucien."

He groaned against her neck and added a little more pressure.

"Fuck me, Lucien."

He pulled back and stared into her ecstasy-covered face.

"Fuck me right here, where anyone could see us." She grabbed his biceps, curled her nails into his flesh, and he hissed out. "Anyone could look through the window and see you fucking me so hard." She slid her hands up his neck and grabbed the back of his head. "I'd want to scream so loud because it feels so good, but you'd cover my mouth to muffle the sound."

He was breathing harder at this burst of eroticism from his woman. "Goddammit, Callie." He was so hard, so turned on for her. Right when he reached between their bodies, unbuttoned his jeans, and slid his zipper down, the sound of footsteps coming closer had him lifting his head from the crook of her neck. Before he could move or put her on the ground, Kink walked in. Kink had his head down, his focus on his cell, but when he walked into the meeting room he looked up. For several seconds, all the three of them did was stand there frozen.

Lucien couldn't move, despite knowing that he should have put Callie down. It was like he didn't know what the fuck to do for the first time in his life. Kink stared between Lucien and Callie.

"Dad," Callie said softly, shocked and frightened, and so damn vulnerable that Lucien wanted to put her behind the protection of his body, and make sure none of this blew back on her.

And then all fucking hell broke loose as Kink's face contorted into a mask of pure rage. He slammed his phone down on the ground, shattering the cell, and charged forward toward Lucien with murder in his eyes.

****

Lucien had pushed her aside when Kink had come forward. Callie had never seen her dad so upset, and she had seen him pissed plenty of times.

Callie moved back another foot when her dad started throwing fists out left and right. Lucien was blocking them, not even defending himself, and she knew he wouldn't fight her father. Kink was a machine when it came to attacking Lucien, and she felt helpless to stop them.

"Dad!" She shouted, but the grunts and curses were too loud for them to hear her.

"How long have you been fucking my daughter behind my back?" Kink grunted out, and swung out. He connected with the side of Lucien, and she cried out, wanting them to stop so she could explain.

"Please, God, Dad, please stop." She pleaded, but her words fell on deaf ears.

"Kink, brother, please let me explain."

"You're not my brother. A brother, and friend, wouldn't fucking do this behind my back," Kind growled out. "You and I have nothing to talk about." Kink swung out, but Lucien grabbed her dad's fist before he slammed it into his face.

"We called you to the club today to tell you, Kink. We wanted to tell you yesterday, but the baby news deterred us." Lucien grunted out when Kink went after him again, but Lucien pushed her dad back. Kink stood there, breathing heavily, his body looking tight and strained, and the anger on his face tangible.

"So instead of waiting for me to show up you decide pinning my daughter up against the fucking wall and touching her like she's yours was the right move?" Kink growled out, and cracked his knuckles. "She's my fucking daughter, Lucien. My *eighteen*-year-old daughter. You're over twice her age. Callie's a goddamned baby compared to you."

Kink started to pace, his emotions wild and turbulent, and Callie couldn't help the tears that started to come forth. She wanted to be strong, needed to be strong right now, but seeing her dad and the man she loved going head-to-head, all because of what she wanted with Lucien, and what they had done, broke her heart.

Kink stopped pacing and looked at her when she sniffed back her tears. "Daddy, I swear we didn't mean to hurt anyone. We didn't mean to do anything behind anyone's back." She looked at Lucien, and when he stared at her there was this pained expression on his face.

"Callie baby, please don't cry," Lucien said softly, but the sound of her father cursing and growling out at the same time had them both looking over at Kink.

He charged forward again, his face red with rage, and tackled Lucien to the ground. Their big, muscular bodies crashed against the meeting table, and the heavy wood tipped over, barely missing her in the process. She was pressed to the wall, watching in horror as her dad clocked Lucien over and over again in the face, but Lucien still refused to raise a hand at Kink.

"I won't fight you, brother," Lucien said and then grunted out when Kink slammed his fist into his side.

As her father and Kink went at it, mainly her dad slamming his fist into any available inch of Lucien he could reach and Lucien blocking him, she heard the front doors of the clubhouse open. The crashing of chairs hitting the walls from the force of the fight, the noise of fists hitting flesh, and grunts filling the air, was a horrible, nightmarish experience.

"Oh shit." Two prospects were now standing in the open doorway of the meeting room, their faces a mask of shock as they looked at their President and VP of the club fighting brutally.

Lucien shoved Kink away again. "Kink, brother, please stop this. Let me explain, because I'm not going to fucking fight you."

Her father didn't care, or wasn't thinking clearly, because he charged forward like a damn rhino intent on taking a tank down. Callie screamed when her father and Lucien hit the wall beside her, knocking the pictures of fallen members onto the ground. Glass shattered, and the sound of crunching under her feet filled her head. She didn't think and just moved forward. She was stupid for trying to stop her dad, but right now she wasn't thinking and just reacting.

Callie reached out to her dad, grabbed his cut, and tried to pull Kink back, but he was as big and powerful as a brick wall. She tugged harder, screamed out his name to get his attention, but the force of their fighting had her falling backward and hitting her hip on the side of the meeting table. Hissing out as pain sliced up her side, she pushed it aside and stared at the two men she loved more than anything. Kink, her dad, was always there for her, and protected her with his life. And then there was Lucien, the MC President that she had fallen so hard for, and was so in love with that she couldn't even think straight.

"You fucking asshole," Lucien yelled out and pushed Kink away. He came toward Callie, seeing that she was hurt.

"Get your fucking hands off of her!" Kink shouted.

Lucien pulled her behind him again, had his hand on her hip, and held her close to his back. "I'm not giving her up, Kink. I fucking love her, and you and I need to talk about this."

"She isn't yours, Lucien. She'll never be yours." Blood marred her father's lip from when he was pushed away and slammed into the wall.

She looked at Lucien's face, well, as much as she could see, and saw his busted lip, and the bruising and swelling under his left eye.

"Out of all of the women in the world, in this damn town, why in the hell did you have to go after my daughter?"

The two of them stared at each other, the silence thick and intense.

"We didn't plan any of this, Kink. Fuck, I tried to stay away, but I love her, and we honest to God meant to tell you before this. We didn't want you finding out this way."

"What, you mean you wanted to tell me after you betrayed me by being with my little girl?" Kink growled out.

Lucien growled out. "I won't fight you, but watch your damn mouth regarding Callie, Kink." Lucien sounded intense, dangerous, and squeezed her hip gently. "This is Callie we are talking about. I might not fight you over this, because I have been in the wrong, but I will beat your ass if you say anything else about her." He turned his head and spit out a mouthful of blood. Lucien ran the back of his arm across his lips, looked down and saw the red covering his forearm and sighed in defeat. "I meant no disrespect, brother, really I didn't. I also didn't plan this shit. It just happened." He growled out the words, and she felt the anger come from Lucien.

Kink looked at Lucien with narrowed eyes. His chest was rising and falling fast, and her father clenched and unclenched his hands at his sides. "Don't fucking preach to me about what to say and what not to say concerning my daughter." He rolled his head around on his neck, and made this low sound in his throat. "You may have meant no disrespect, but you sure as hell didn't care about any of that while you were with Callie and knowing that she is my daughter, Lucien." Kink exhaled, turned his back to them, and ran a hand over his short dark hair.

She moved away from Lucien, and when he tried to stop her, gently pulling her back toward him, she placed a hand on his and shook her head.

"Dad," she said softly and moved closer to him. "Pease don't be upset. We honestly didn't plan for this to happen, and didn't mean for this to be done behind your back." He turned around, and the anger left his expression as pain took its place. "But I'm an adult and know what I want, and who I want to be with."

"If you would have come to me, told me how you felt about Lucien, I would have been pissed, yeah, but you're my baby girl, Callie. I would have supported you if you were truly happy." He looked at Lucien, and that pain that had been on his face morphed again to anger. "But you fucked with my daughter, Lucien, and no amount of excuses is going to change the fact that you messed with what is mine. You betrayed me." Kink looked at Callie again. "I thought we were close enough that you could talk to me about anything without fear."

He shook his head, and without saying anything else he left the room. He shoved the prospects out of his way, saying curses under his breath, and then the sound of the front door of the clubhouse slamming shut rang through.

115

The silence was deafening. She wanted to chase after her dad, explain that this wasn't how she wanted things to be. But she knew this was how it would end up, and thus why she hadn't told him. Kink would have freaked out even if they hadn't seen each other, even if she had waited to be with Lucien in any capacity.

"I need to go to him, to make this right, Lucien," she said, sobbing now because she was angry with herself for letting it get like this. "We should have stayed away from each other until we told him.' She wiped away her tears angrily, hating herself so much right now. She had hurt her dad.

"Baby," Lucien said softly, pushed her hair over one shoulder, and kissed her nape. Closing her eyes tight, more tears fell down her cheeks. She was upset, angry, sad, and hated herself with a passion that probably rivaled her father's emotions right now.

"He hates me, Lucien." She was turned around, and they stared at each other.

"Kink doesn't hate you. He loves you, Callie baby. He's your father, and not even being with a fucked up biker like me, one that went behind his back and is in love with his daughter, will make him ever stop loving you." He cupped both of her cheeks, leaned down, and kissed her softly. "Now, he really fucking hates me, but I'll make it right. I *have* to make it right because I can't lose him, and I sure as hell am not going to let you go."

Closing her eyes and rested her forehead on his chest, she breathed out, not even knowing where to start with making this right with her dad.

"I love you, Callie." He pulled her closer and cupped the back of her head, holding her to his chest.

"I love you, too, Lucien," she said and gripped the sleeves of his shirt.

"Oh. Shit," one of the prospects said.

Lucien didn't move away from holding her, and said, "Shut the fuck up, and get the hell out of here."

One of the most important rules of the brothers, a code of sorts that the members lived by, was not to mess with family, but to treat them as their own. And Lucien had done the opposite, had been with her in a way that was forbidden. Hell, she had done it, too, was just as much to "blame" in this as he was, and she needed to make it right.

Chapter Twelve

Callie pulled her car into the driveway of her dad's house hours after she had left the clubhouse. She had needed to think, needed to try to figure out how in the hell to make this right. She was actually surprised to see Kink's Harley parked in front of the house. She had assumed he would have left, driven around to clear his head, drink away his anger, or just get away from everything. She knew she would have done any of those if she had been in his situation. God, her dad was such a good man, and so didn't deserve this feeling of betrayal, and although they hadn't meant to hurt him, he was devastatingly hurt. She had seen it in his face. But Lucien was a good man also, and she hated that he was hurting too, because he thought he betrayed his friend. Scrubbing her hand over her face, she breathed out, rested her head on the back of the seat, and prayed everything worked out.

"It has to work out," she whispered.

Getting out of the car she moved up the front steps and into the house. Everything was pretty quiet, but then she heard the sound of a bottle clanking against a glass. She went into the kitchen, and saw her dad leaning against the counter with a bottle of liquor in one hand and a square cut glass in the other. He stared at the ground and then looked at her. He didn't say anything, and neither did she. He brought the cup to his mouth, and took a long sip from it. Keeping his eyes locked on her from over the rim of his glass, she felt herself want to move closer, but was afraid to. Of course she wasn't afraid of her dad, but she was frightened of this situation, and of making things worse.

He turned away from her, set the bottle on the counter, but refilled his glass before he faced her again.

"Let me explain," she said softly. "I love him, Dad."

He shook his head, looking defeated. "I don't think there is much to explain, Callie. It's pretty obvious what was going on," he said low and deep, and without any emotion. She could handle him angry, could handle the shouting, disappointment even, but what she couldn't handle was her dad shutting her out because he was so upset he couldn't show emotion.

"I just wish things had not gone down the way they had, because I swear to God we didn't mean to hurt anyone."

Kink exhaled, looked at the ground, and didn't speak for several seconds. "Did he force you into anything, pressure you?" He glanced at her.

She knitted her brows. "What?" She shook her head, so confused as to what he was getting at. "Why would you think he pressured me into anything?"

He shook his head, took a swig of his liquor, and stared at her. "Callie, I'm trying to think of a good reason why I am not going back to that clubhouse and killing Lucien for putting his hands on you. Right now I am hanging on by a thread." He turned from her, braced his hands on the counter, and she swore he started grinding his teeth. "Did he fucking force you to do anything?" Kink asked, and she curled her hands into fists at the thought.

"I can't believe you would think that after I told you I loved him." She said it so softly she didn't think he had heard, but when her dad lifted his head, this pained expression on his face, she knew he had heard her just fine.

Before he could respond the sound of the front doors opening told her that Cookie was home. She came into the kitchen a few minutes later, the bags she carried moving against her legs with every step she took.

"Kink, honey, can you get the rest of the bags from the car?"

Callie looked over at Cookie as she entered the kitchen, her focus on the shopping bags in her hands. She stopped, glanced up, and when she looked between Kink and then Callie, the realization of what was happening moved across her face.

"I take it because of the angry atmosphere and this weird, awkward intensity in here, that you know?" she said to Kink.

"You knew about this, Cookie?" Kink said loudly, looking between her and Cookie. She could tell he was growing angrier by the second by the fact his face was red, his body was strung tight, and he looked ready to destroy something.

"Dad, don't yell at her, and don't get pissed at Cookie. I just told her yesterday, kind of inadvertently." Callie grabbed her hair, tugged gently on the strands, and wished that this weirdness were gone.

"How long?" he asked in a low, deadly voice.

"What do you mean?" Oh, Callie knew what he was talking about, but she was nervous by this situation.

"You know what I'm talking about, Callie."

When she didn't respond right away he exhaled roughly.

"How long have you and Lucien been…" He didn't finish his sentence.

"Two weeks."

He bared his teeth and cursed out.

"But he picked me up from a party three months ago." She looked at Cookie, saw the uncomfortable expression on the other woman's face, and knew she needed to just spit it out. "I was at a party, pretty drunk, not knowing how to get home, and I accidently called Lucien."

Kink said slowly, "You accidently called Lucien? Can you explain to me how in the fuck that happens."

"Kink, please watch your damn language."

Callie could have laughed at the fact Cookie told her dad to watch his language while cursing, but right now laughing would probably be taken the wrong way, and make this situation so much worse.

"Yes, I *accidently* called him. I was drunk, didn't want to call you, or Mom." She swallowed past the lump of emotion in her throat at the mention of her mother. "I meant to call a friend, but I ended up calling Lucien instead." She ran her hands over her thighs feeling her fingers shake, and her palms start to sweat. "He came and got me and took me to his place."

"He what?" Kink said so low, so menacingly, that Callie felt chills race up her spine. "And I guess you knew about this, too?" He directed the question at Cookie.

Cookie glanced at Callie, but before Cookie could speak Kink was talking again.

"What were you thinking?"

Callie curled her hands into fists. "I was thinking that he was a member of The Brothers, that I trusted him, and that he would not let anything hurt me." She swallowed, saw Cookie do the same as her throat worked, and then looked at her dad. "I slept in the spare bedroom, *alone*, and he was a gentleman. He wanted to call you right away, to tell you all of it, but I asked him not to. I wanted to tell you myself, and then I just never did it. Mom died, and then things got hectic." She ran her hand on her thighs. "I know that's not an excuse, but it's the truth. Nothing happened until two weeks ago when he came up to campus to make sure I was okay after you told him I was going to a party." She shrugged. "I guess he pictured me in the same situation as before." Kink didn't say anything at first, but then he grabbed the bottle of liquor and threw it against the wall. The amber colored alcohol slid to the ground, and pieces of glass littered the floor and wall. Cookie took a step back, and so did Callie. She had never seen this kind of anger in her father, not personally.

"I'm sorry. I didn't mean to scare you guys," he said softly, but his voice was still hard. He looked a Callie. "You slept with him," he stated.

"Kink, not appropriate—"

"No, Cookie, it is really fucking appropriate. I have the right to know if the President of my club is sleeping with my daughter. My very young eighteen-year-old daughter."

"We really had planned on telling you everything yesterday, but then you dropped the baby bombshell, and we obviously didn't think that saying we were in a … relationship … or whatever it is we are in, was the best thing at the moment."

She had never been in this kind of situation with her father before, and she hated it. Callie had the best relationship with him, had always been comfortable with being honest with anything she had going on, but with this she hadn't said a thing, and because of that she had lost his trust and earned his disappointment.

"Motherfucking hell."

"Kink," Cookie gritted out, and Callie knew that the only person that could possibly, maybe, get through to her dad and have him seeing that this was her life and her decision was his old lady.

He turned from them, ran his hand through his black hair, and messed up the short strands. The fact he was pacing told Callie that he was irritated, on edge, and that nothing would probably get solved or worked out today. And then he stopped and looked at her, his face a mask of indifference, and struggle.

"I can't talk about this right now, because I want to hate Lucien, want to go to the club and beat his fucking ass again. He's my club President, the man I look at as a brother, and what he did with you, *is* doing with you..." He shook his head. "It goes against everything the club stands for. He knows better than to be with you, Callie. You're too young for him." He ground his teeth, his jaw getting hard from his rage. "He's old enough to be your damn father." He looked disgusted at the thought, and she was so mad at that comment that she knew she couldn't stay quiet.

"Dad, you have no room to talk. Cookie is only a few years older than me, and you're as old as Lucien. Did you care what anyone thought?" She didn't wait for him to respond. "No, because you love her, and isn't that what matters?"

He still didn't respond, and when he cursed low and long, and stared between her and Cookie, Callie knew he wasn't going to see her side just yet.

"This is fucked up, and I can't be here right now. I'm not just going to let it be okay, Callie. I can't. I don't know if I ever can be." He grabbed his keys off the counter, and walked past them.

Callie was going to go after him, but Cookie grabbed her hand and stopped her.

"No, honey, just let him go right now. He needs to be alone."

Callie knew he needed sometime to process all of this, but what she worried about was that he wasn't leaving to be alone, but to go finish what he had started with Lucien at the clubhouse. And the thing was, Lucien wouldn't fight back, wouldn't lay a hand on Kink, and therefore would get beyond fucked up.

****

The whole club knew by now about him and Callie, and it had only been hours since all the shit with Kink had gone down. Lucien slammed back another drink, breathed out through the burn, and looked around at the members that were winding down from their run earlier this week. The members had come back from the club run, their attitudes positive, and the back of the van filled with guns they had traded. But when they found out what the hell had happened, this eerie kind of tension filled the clubhouse. They hadn't even needed to see Lucien's busted lip and eye, or the bruises he was sporting to know what the hell had gone down. The prospects had filled them in. Not like they didn't have a right to know, but this was an inside matter, one Lucien would have liked to tell the guys himself. But right now he didn't care about anything aside from getting this matter straightened out so he could be with Callie. He loved Kink like family, but he wasn't going to give up on Callie either. She had changed him for the better. He could feel it inside of him, and if that meant he was in a bad place right now with Kink, then he'd have to work through it. They would get through this, because they were family, bonded by a vow of brotherhood that went far beyond anything else.

And you fucked that up.

He slammed back another shot, feeling the alcohol burn the cut on his lip.

"Hey, man," Cain said and slipped into the seat beside him. Lucien lifted his shot glass to the man in response, but didn't look at him. He tapped the bottom of the glass on the counter to get the attention of the prospect. Once he was refilled, he drank that one down, too.

"You're the first one to come talk to me. I think the others are afraid I'll snap."

"Well, the prospects told us everything when the guys saw the state of the meeting room, and noticed the tire marks on the driveway. Hell, they practically beat the information out of them," Cain said and started laughing. He took the beer from the prospect, took a sip from the bottle, and then set it down. "Want to talk about it, man?"

The feeling of his cell vibrating had Lucien grabbing it out of the front of his cut and staring at the screen. It was a text from Callie, and it wasn't good.

Callie: *Tried 2 talk 2 him...yeah, no go. He took off, and was really pissed. Not sure if he is heading there. God, I hate this, Lucien.*

Lucien: *It's okay, baby. I'll make sure it's okay. I love you.*

Fuck, he wanted to be there for her, to hold her, promise her everything would be okay, but he couldn't make that kind of guarantee until he straightened things out with Kink.

"Yo, Lucien. You want to talk about it?"

He finished typing out the reply text and put his cell back in his cut. He faced Cain so the man could see his face full on, and then stared at him right in the eyes. "Does it look like I want to talk about it?" he said without any emotion.

Cain lifted his hands in surrender, and then the sound of tires squealing, and of a Harley engine rumbling, had Lucien rising. All of the other members rose as well, and then through the clubhouse window, he saw Kink getting off his bike and all but charging toward the front of the clubhouse.

"Shit," Lucien said, grabbed his shot glass, and drank down the liquor. He'd need it for what was about to happen.

Kink slammed open the front doors, searched around the room until he stopped his gaze right on Lucien, and then growled out like he was some kind of animal. Kink charged toward him, and when Lucien saw some of the members come forward, he held his hand out. "No, let him come."

Kink charged forward, slammed into Lucien, and the two of them fell to the ground. Lucien wasn't going to fight Kink on this, because the other man had a right to vengeance, especially since he had been wronged. What he had with Callie, what Lucien *felt* for Callie, wasn't wrong. It was the rightest fucking thing on this goddamned planet, but if it were the other way around Lucien would want to beat someone's ass, too.

Kink hit Lucien in the jaw, and the flavor of blood spilled across his tongue. "You motherfucker. You lied to me for three months." Kink hit him again and again, and all Lucien did was lie there and take it.

"Shit, this is screwed up," one of the members said, but Lucien couldn't tell who it was.

"Hit me back. Fight me, Lucien." Kink spat out, and hit him in the gut. He got off Lucien, hauled him up by the shirt, and pushed him up against the bar. "You have been seeing her for *two* fucking weeks, took her home months ago without calling and telling me." Kink cracked his knuckles, wiped the spit from his mouth, and stared at Lucien with hatred. "I trusted you, and you went after my baby girl, preyed on her like some kind of fucking animal because you couldn't keep your dick in your pants."

Lucien growled out, hating the fact Kink was spitting out these foul words, and although he told himself to shut his mouth and not go after Kink, he could only promise the latter. "Watch your damn mouth, Kink. She isn't just a piece of ass to me. I want her as my old lady."

There was chorus of hushed murmurs from the men standing by, but Lucien kept his focus on his VP.

Kink moved forward again, and they crashed against the bar as one entity. Glasses shattered to the ground, spilled beer littered the floor and counter, and Kink hit him right in the damn eye.

"Out of all the fucking women in the world you went after one of my own."

Lucien went to roll out from under Kink, but the other man hit him in the right kidney, and then moved to the left kidney. Kink grabbed him by the collar, turned him around, and tossed him against the table. The wood fell to the ground, and so did Lucien.

"We need to stop this," Tuck said.

"No, don't fucking interfere," Cain said before Lucien could get the words out. "The prez said back off, and that is what we do."

"How could you, Lucien?" Kink said, and although his punches were pretty fucking powerful, his energy was waning.

"I love you like my family, Kink, but I am in love with Callie, and I won't let her go," Lucien said, blood spilling into his eyes from the cut on his forehead and blurring his vision. "I'd kill for her, fucking *die* for her, Kink. I was in the wrong, so much in the wrong for keeping this from you, but I can't stay away from her. I *won't* stay away. If you beating the shit out of me gets us back where we were, then do it, brother, because I won't fight you on this."

Chapter Thirteen

Kink stopped throwing punches at the sound of Lucien's words. Blood was everywhere, mainly from the President, but Kink's knuckles were raw and spilt open, and bleeding like a bastard. He stared at Lucien, at the man he had known for years, would lay down his life for, and would kill for. This man had been with him during thick or thin, and when he had needed someone to talk to, or someone to handle business in any capacity, Lucien had been there. Kink looked around the room, at the men that stood in a circle staring at the violence that had erupted within their brotherhood walls. Their cuts showed their loyalty, spoke of their determination to have a tightly knit family of men who handled anything and everything that came their way. There were these horrified, shocked, and confused expressions on their faces. They had seen their VP and President going at it like enemies.

He looked down at Lucien again, the man he had considered a brother even though the same blood didn't run through their veins. His blood was everywhere, and his face beaten to shit, but he watched Kink with a hard, unbreakable expression. Kink got off Lucien, looked down at his hands, and saw the broken, bloody skin from punching his President.

God, he had snapped, just let loose because he hadn't been able to control himself. And here was Lucien, able to handle his own against anyone and anything that was a threat, but instead of fighting back he had taken it all. And for what, to prove that he knew he was in the wrong and that he deserved it all? Well he had, he had deserved all of that and more, but he had admitted to it all, taken it like a man, and how in the hell was Kink supposed to continue beating his ass when he just lay there surrendering?

He held his hand out to Lucien, and after a second he grabbed it. Kink helped him off the ground, but he didn't want to talk about shit right now, didn't want to do this either. He stared at Lucien, and then turned and headed out the front door. Once outside he closed his eyes and inhaled deeply. There was the faint smell of exhaust in the air from a car that had just driven by, the sound of music in the distance from the prospects that had been helping repair a bike in the garage, and the silence yet strength that was ever-present from the clubhouse.

Reaching inside of his cut, he cursed when he came up empty handed for some smokes. Yeah, he had quit, which was a good thing, but right now he needed some nicotine or even booze, or hell, a joint to help him calm the fuck down.

"Need one of these?"

Kink closed his eyes for a second when he heard Lucien's voice behind him. He looked over his shoulder, saw the other man standing by the front doors lighting a cigarette of his own, and then he gave one short nod to the Brothers' President. Lucien stepped closer, handed the pack to Kink, and the two of them stood side-by-side for several seconds, neither speaking. Lucien was still bloody, but it looked like he had taken a rag to his face and cleaned off a lot of the blood. His lip was fucked up and split, his eye nearly swollen shut, and the bruises were pretty fucking horrendous. Despite all of this, and the reason Kink had come here and laid his hands on Lucien, he felt bad for making the other man look like he had been run over by a Mack truck.

For a few moments the only sound between them was of inhaling and exhaling. And then Lucien took one last hit, snubbed the cigarette out on the ground, and crossed his arms over his chest. Lucien was a big man, tall and muscular, and matching Kink in height and weight, but there had always been this strength that came from the leader of their club, this silence that spoke of his power. He led their club with an iron fist, knew when to stop, and when to move forward, and Kink had always been proud to call him a friend, a brother, and a leader. But then all of this shit had gone down, and Kink was lost in this limbo, not knowing how to proceed. A part of him wanted Callie to be happy, no matter who she chose to be with in life. But then another part of him said that this wasn't okay, and how could he ever go along with it?

He glanced at Lucien, watched as the other man stared off into the distance, and knew that he was about to speak by the way his jaw clenched tightly.

"I meant it when I said I won't let her go." Lucien looked at Kink then. "I'm in love with her, so fucking gone for Callie that I can't think straight, see straight, and know that no other woman will do it for me ever again." Lucien exhaled, looked down at the ground for a few seconds, and when he looked at Kink again there was this honesty on the man's face. "I've never loved anyone the way I love her. She makes me see that not everything in this world has a hard edge and needs to be put in its place. She's made me see that I am a better person because of *her*." The silence stretched out between them for a few seconds before Lucien started speaking again. "I know you have to know what I mean, what I feel, because when I see you look at Cookie, I know that is how I look a Callie. We look at them as if there is nothing in this world that can bring us down as long as they are by our sides."

Lucien faced forward again, and although Kink didn't respond, didn't know what to say, he knew that Lucien was right.

"I'll say it again, because what I did was wrong on every level, and I deserved everything you gave me. But I want you to understand that what I feel for your daughter is real. I know you need time to process all of this, to understand it even, and I can give you that time." Lucien looked at him again. "I also understand that you may never be okay with me being with her. But I can't let her go, Kink. I won't let her go, because I am totally, madly fucking in love with Callie." They stared at each other for a moment, and then Lucien nodded once and turned and left to head back into the clubhouse.

Kink was left standing there alone, deciding whether he wanted to be okay with his daughter being with Lucien, or say fuck it all and accept what was happening, and that Callie was growing up and able to make her own decisions. But there was a part of him, the father part, that wanted to pack up his family, move away, and leave the club and everything else behind because he wanted to protect her. Of course he could never leave his club, because this was his life, his world, and his family was rooted here. He couldn't just run away from his problems because for the first time in his life he felt lost and not in control. He looked at the clubhouse, felt the love he had for those men inside, and knew this was one of the hardest things he'd ever have to face in his life. This hit close to home, and therefore went straight to his heart.

****

Three days later

"Give him some time. I love you, and I swear that this will work out. It has to work out. I am not letting you go, Callie. If there was ever anything in this world is

worth fighting for it is being with you. I am here, no matter what, and will never leave you behind no matter what."

Callie listened to the voicemail Lucien had left three days ago. After she had told her dad about them, found out he had gone to the clubhouse again and attacked Lucien, and then also found out that day that Lucien had just sat there and taken it, she knew that all of this had gotten so far into a what-the-fuck level that she couldn't even comprehend it anymore. She loved Lucien. God did she love him. It had been Lucien's decision to spend a few days apart, to give her dad some time to get used to the idea of them being together, and come to understand how important being together really was. She still talked to Lucien daily, yearned to have him close, to have the scent of him surround her, and his big body holding her tight. He made her feel safe, protected, and that wasn't a feeing she wanted to get rid of.

But she loved her father as well, and knowing that she had hurt him, done things behind his back with a man that he was pretty much family with, hurt her on a totally different level.

She listened to the message once more, feeling this pang of hurt in her heart at the sincerity in his voice. She didn't want to spend time apart, but she sure as hell wasn't about to flaunt her relationship with Lucien in front of her dad. But being away from Lucien was hard. Really. And it wasn't because they had only had sex that once. They actually spoke to each other, maybe not deep, intellectual conversations, but things that were important to them. And Lucien was different with her. She saw how he was with the other members, how he kept this calm, cool, and hard composure that said he wouldn't put up with any shit. But with her he was softer in the way he spoke to her, gentler in the way he stared at her. He was a definite hard-ass that others feared, but all she felt from him was love and trust.

Tossing her phone on the bed, she started putting her clothing in her duffle bag. She was heading back out tomorrow evening to the university. She had declined Lucien's offer to take her when he had asked, not because she didn't want him to, but because she was hoping her dad would want to take her so they could talk about all of this. She had cried more times in the last three days than she had in her entire life. Although she was an adult, and she knew she had every right to be with the man she loved, she had also done something that was reprehensible in the MC community.

But she refused to let go of Lucien, and she knew he would not let her leave him either. She felt, for the first time in her life, that she had found the person she was meant to be with. Who cared if she was so much younger than he was? Who cared if for the last three months they had been going through this tug and pull with each other? There was no doubt in her mind that people had talked about the fact she was young and impressionable, even naive a little. Hell, her dad had even said that Lucien had taken advantage of her. Of course that was a load of shit, and she knew that he was aware of that fact, too. She was a no-nonsense girl, and certainly didn't let other people tell her what she wanted or didn't want.

Callie knew what she wanted in her life, and for her future. And that was being happy with Lucien, and having her family be okay with it.

She turned and grabbed a small stack of jeans, and put them in her bag. Her dad and Cookie were downstairs, and although the nonexistent conversations she had with Kink were to be expected, she wished that he'd understand her side, too. Sighing in an almost defeated tone, she looked around her room. There were a few boxes left that held her things, and a couple downstairs that were ready to be packed in the SUV. She obviously wouldn't take anything that wasn't of importance, because she'd be sharing a dorm room with Meredith.

"You nearly packed?" Her dad's voice came from behind her, and her heart instantly started pounding.

She turned around to see him standing in the doorway, leaning against the frame with his arms crossed, and looking around her room. He wore a pair of jeans and a plain t-shirt, and his feet were bare. Even when he was looking so casual, she knew the real man Kink Roberts was, the biker that was dangerous and intimidating, and stuck to his guns when he was being pressured. But when he stared at her there was just a man that was looking at his daughter, trying to get past the last three days of revelations, pain, and anger.

Clearing her throat, she nodded. This was the most he had said to her since he had stormed out of the kitchen and gone back to fight Lucien. "Yeah, last bag." She pointed to the duffle bag on her bed.

He nodded and pushed away from the frame. Kink walked into the room, and then sat on the edge of her bed. After he pushed her bag away, he patted the mattress, gesturing for her to sit beside him. She stared at him for a moment, took in his short black hair that was styled in a faux hawk, looked into his bright blue eyes that were the same color as hers, and knew that this man's opinion meant so much to her. Callie sat beside him and shifted her body so she was facing him. For a second he just stared around her room again, taking everything in apparently, or maybe he was gathering his thoughts, and then looked at her.

"You love him." He stated it without any hatred, anger, or malice in his voice.

Callie nodded. "I do, Dad."

He glanced down at his hands in his lap. "You understand why I got so angry?"

"Yeah, I do, but we really didn't mean to hurt or betray anyone intentionally."

He nodded again. "Yeah, I understand that, baby girl, and I didn't mean to blow the fuck up in front of you and Cookie, but I just kind of snapped."

"I know, but I wish you wouldn't have gone after Lucien the way you did." When she noticed how hard his jaw went she regretted saying his name. "But can you understand where I'm coming from?"

He didn't respond for several seconds, and then he nodded, grabbed her hand, and gave it a squeeze. "Yeah, baby girl, I know where you're coming from, and although it'll be hard for me to accept that my little girl is a woman now, and can make her own decisions, I know you have a good head on your shoulders." He lifted his hand and brushed a stray piece of hair from her forehead. "But you're smart, tough, and don't take shit from anyone." He leaned in and kissed her on the forehead. "I love you, sweetheart, and I want you to be happy. If being with Lucien means that you smile, and that you never have a sad day, then who am I to stand in the way of that?" He smiled down at her. "I also know that if there was a man that I wanted you to be with, that would protect you as fiercely as I would, that man would be Lucien." He glanced down at his feet. "I know that he loves you, too. I could see it in the way he looked at you, talked about you, and wouldn't fight me back. It's hard for me to come to terms with that, sweetheart." He looked at her again. "It's hard for me not to see the little girl with the black ponytails, smiling up at me with a missing front tooth, and those big beautiful blue eyes, and calling out my name because you wanted to go faster on the swings."

She leaned into him, and he pulled her closer and wrapped his arms around her shoulders. "I'll always be your little girl, Daddy." She tightened her hold on his waist. "But I'm grown up now, and know what I want in life. I know I want to get my business degree, and to be with the club afterwards." She felt him nod. "But I need you to be okay with it, because you are my world, and I can't stand the idea that you're mad at me."

"Oh, baby girl." He pulled her back and cupped her cheeks. "I'm not mad at you. I could never be angry with you. I just worry."

She smiled. "You don't have to worry so much."

He nodded and pulled her in for a hug again. "I am realizing that, sweetheart." They stayed silent for a moment, just holding each other, and she had missed this with her father. "Just don't put up with any shit from him."

She started chuckling. He was accepting this, or at least trying to, and that was a start. That was all she could ask for.

****

"You're doing the right thing, Kink," Cookie said from behind him. He stood at the kitchen widow, and watched the taillights of Callie's car disappear down the street.

"I hope you're right." He hated that his little girl wasn't little anymore. She might only be eighteen, but she was an adult, a young woman that knew what she wanted in life, and didn't take shit from anyone. Yes, it was really damn hard to think that his daughter was with the President of his MC, but since finding out he had done a lot of thinking. He had beaten the shit out of Lucien, torn up the man that had been his family for longer than he could even remember.

"All I can think about is Callie as a child and Lucien as this dirty old fucking man that took advantage of my little girl."

"You know that's not right," Cookie said, and he turned around and stared at her. "If that's the case then you're a dirty old man, too." She grinned and walked up to him. He hugged her, wrapped his arms around her body, pulled her close, and kept her there.

"I know that's not the case, but that was my first thought and reaction. Now that I've thought about it these last few days, realized that Callie has her own life to lead, and that Lucien will take care of her with his life, I know that I can't stop this."

Cookie tilted her head back and stared at him. "I don't know about the brotherhood code of loyalty, or anything like that, but what I do know that if there was one man on this world that you trusted to treat your daughter with respect, and protect her with his life, who would it be?"

He didn't even need to think about it, didn't need to picture his daughter with anyone else. "Lucien. I would want her to be with a man like Lucien."

Cookie nodded and leaned into him again. "Age is just a number, but family is family, and love is love, Kink. Aside from you, there isn't a man on this planet that will care, protect, or lay his life down for a woman like Lucien will for Callie."

She was right, she was always right, and he knew that he needed to let Callie live her life the way she wanted to.

Chapter Fourteen

Callie had gone to the club first, thinking he might be there doing paperwork, but she hadn't seen his SUV or his Harley parked outside. And then she had heard the pounding bass from the clubhouse, saw a few of the club whores heading out with a few members wrapped around their bodies like a pretzel, and Callie hadn't even gotten out of the car. She could have just called him and asked where Lucien was, but the truth was she was over the moon that her father had spoken with her. She was leaving for school tomorrow evening, and although she'd be coming home on the weekends and would see Lucien then, she wanted this time with him now.

The smile on her face was actually starting to get painful, but the words her dad had spoken to her just an hour before replayed in her mind over and over again.

"I love you, sweetheart, and I want you to be happy. If being with Lucien means that you smile, then who am I to stand in the way of that? Honestly, I couldn't have asked for a better man that will protect you with his life. I may not be one-hundred percent on board with this, only because I'll need some time to get used to my baby girl with the club President, but I want you to be happy."

She pulled into Lucien's driveway, cut the engine, and stared at his place. The sun had set, and the light in the living room was brightly lit with a yellow glow. She got out of the car and headed up to his place. But before she could get to the door or even knock on it Lucien had it opened. He stood in the entryway, no shirt on, his tattooed chest on full display, and his sweats hanging low on his hips. That V of muscle was on clear display, and with the light silhouetting his profile the muscles on his big body were pronounced. She missed his touch, longed for his mouth on her, and just missed him in general. But she couldn't stop staring at his face, one that was bruised, cut in some places, and was swollen.

He stepped aside, and she went inside, instantly feeling the memory of being here with him, even if it had been innocent. She remembered his place well enough, remembered the smell of it, the feel of the carpet beneath her feet, and the sight of Lucien coming out of his room in nothing but his pants on. God, he had looked so good that day, and she was so stunned that it had been three months since all of that crap had gone down.

"Baby," Lucien said and shut the door behind him, sealing them in. They stared at each other for several seconds.

"Are you okay?" she said, feeling her throat tighten at the thought of her dad doing this to him.

"I'm good." He smiled. "Not that I'm not happy to see you, because I really fucking am, but what are you doing here? I thought we were going to wait to see each other until Kink was a little calmer?"

Callie didn't say anything, didn't even think about what she was doing until she started walking toward him. She wrapped her arms around his waist and slammed her mouth on his. She kissed him like her life depended on it, like she couldn't live another second of she didn't have this moment with him.

Lucien turned them around so now Callie was the one pressed against the door. He pressed his body to hers, and she felt his hard cock dig into her belly. He cupped her ass with one hand, and with the other held a chunk of her hair in his fist. He kissed her raw and hard, sweeping his tongue inside and claiming her. A moan left her when he sucked her tongue in his mouth and gently dragged his teeth along it. The hand in her hair tightened, sending a sting of pleasurable pain through her scalp, to her breasts, and straight to the center of her pussy.

She broke the kiss, breathing heavily and staring into his liquid silver-grey eyes. "I spoke with my dad, or, well, he spoke with me." She breathed out roughly, so on edge with her arousal that she didn't want to speak, but knowing it was necessary to tell him.

"I can't say he is one-hundred percent okay with all of this, but he accepts what I want and that I'm unbelievably happy with you."

"Callie…" Lucien cupped the side of her face, stared into her eyes, and then grinned. "God, I fucking love you so much." He kissed her again, making her feel possessed, loved, and so damn owned that the entire situation almost felt surreal. And when he lifted her easily into his arms, deepened the kiss, she knew tonight wasn't going to be about soft and slow, but a fierce and fast coupling that put everything else in the dust.

She tightened her legs around his waist and ground herself on his erection. He grunted out and used the leverage he had in her hair to tilt her head back. With her throat arched he broke their kiss and dragged his tongue up her neck, as if marking her as his. God she loved that, loved that he couldn't control himself with her, the same way she couldn't control herself with him.

He shifted his hands so both of them held her ass now, and then he moved one of them up to her hip, and clenched her side for a second. When he slipped it under the hem of her shirt she felt every roughened inch of his fingers on her skin. It felt good to be touched by him, to feel the roughness that covered the tips of his fingers. He ran his teeth up and down her neck, nipped at her flesh, and thrust his erection into her again and again. She didn't want to wait any longer to feel him inside of her. They had already waited too long, and now that her dad was starting to become accepting of this relationship she just wanted to be with the man she loved, and not having to hide any of it.

She was feverish and excited, and all she could think about was how it would feel for him to thrust all those hard inches into her again. Lucien murmured something against her flesh, but it was distorted against the base of her throat. She didn't care about words though. All she wanted was *him*. Moving her hands between their bodies she fumbled to get his sweats off. But in the next instant she was being turned in the air sharply and then set back on her feet. The cold, smooth fabric of his couch pressed to her belly. Jerking her upright he pulled her shirt from her in one swift move, and then tore her bra off. His actions were hard and fast, frantic in their intensity. She loved it all.

A small sound escaped her at the fact he was so worked up that he had torn the material right from her. He had her pants off next, then the feel of his warm, humid breath against the cheeks of her ass told her he was behind her. He grabbed her bottom, massaged the globes until she felt herself pressing back against him. Could he see how wet her panties were? He groaned and palmed her ass right before he ran his nose up and down the crease of her bottom. God, this was so wild, so untamed and unusual for her that she felt herself grow wetter. He was acting like an animal, like a man that couldn't control himself.

"I can't get enough of you. After having a taste of you all those weeks ago, you're all I think about. I want to make you come around me, scream out my name, and know that you're mine, Callie."

She didn't even care that she had obviously spoken out loud.

"I want to go slow, be gentle with you, baby, but I can't tonight. I have to be with you this way. Tell me it's okay," he said against her flesh, and continued to palm her ass.

"I just want *you*, Lucien."

He curled his fingers into her hips and groaned out, and she bit her lip and closed her eyes. He gripped the edge of her thong, and slid it to the side. The air left her when he used his other hand to spread her ass open and proceeded to run his tongue down the slit of her pussy. He sucked and licked, and nipped along her swollen, heated flesh. She was going to come.

"That's it, baby. Come for me. Come all over my mouth." He sucked her clit into his mouth. Lucien hummed around the bundle of nerves until she bit her lip hard enough she tasted blood. The orgasm that tore through her was so intense she panted for breath, and felt sweat start to line her spine and forehead.

"Ask me for it, Callie." He groaned out against her. "Ask me for my cock in your pussy."

Oh. God.

His words were so vulgar and should have turned her off, but this was Lucien, the man that turned her on just by staring at her. "Lucien, please, give it to me."

In the next second he tore her panties off of her and threw them to the side. His rough pants wafted across her back when she felt him step away. Sucking in a great lungful of air, Callie looked over her shoulder and watched him shed his pants. All she could do was stare at what stood big and long from his body.

Taking hold of the root of his cock he stroked it a few times. His gaze jumped from her ass to her eyes. "Spread for me, Callie baby."

Her heart was pounding so hard she couldn't think straight. Reaching behind her she grabbed each cheek and spread them, feeling the cold air in the room, and her heated flesh part. This was obscene, but so hot that she wanted more. She may have been with only one man—this man—but all of this felt so right and good, and she wanted it all.

"This is mine," he said and took a step closer, reached out, and touched her pussy. "This. Is. Mine." He stared into her eyes. "Say it."

She licked her lips. "My pussy is yours."

"Fuck, you're so pink and wet for me." He ran his finger down her slit and pushed it into her pussy. Immediately she clamped down on the digit, and he grunted in approval. Her inner thighs were so sensitive from the scruff along his cheeks when he had eaten her out. He pressed his length between her pussy lips, and a groan spilled from both of them.

That first touch of his cockhead to her pussy sent a thrill up her spine. He rubbed himself over and over against her, up and down and faster and harder until she was moving her ass back against him, pleading without words that she wanted him buried inside of her body.

"You're greedy." There was nothing but strained heat in his words. "You're *my* greedy little thing. You understand?"

She licked her lips. "Yeah, I understand." They stared at each other for several seconds, and the only warning she got before he took her was his nails digging into her flesh. He shoved all of those hard, thick inches into her, and she cried out in pleasure and pain. Her inner muscles clenched along his length, and he grunted.

"You keep doing that and I won't last ten fucking minutes inside of you, baby."

He let go of her waist and spread her cheeks so wide she knew he was watching his cock move in and out of her body. "Fucking hell, Callie. I've been thinking about this since I was deep inside of you last time." He picked up speed and slammed harder into her. "If I hurt you, baby, tell me, because I want you to come so many times you can't even see straight." He slammed into her again and again until she couldn't suck enough air into her lungs. "You're so fucking tight."

Sweat formed on her body, and she felt her orgasm start to churn inside of her, threatening her that what was happening would end far too soon. He worked his dick inside of her in deep, long strokes, and she curled her hands into the couch.

"I'm going to come." She gasped out, and even though she wanted to feel it claim her she didn't want it to end yet.

Droplets of Lucien's sweat landed on her back, and she arched up, wanted it covering her. As if her unspoken desire was spoken out loud Lucien leaned forward so his sweat slicked chest rubbed along her back.

"I want you smelling like me, tasting like me, and having my marks covering your body because I own you." He continued to thrust into her, and she forced herself to hold off on coming. He pumped three more times and then pulled out. Before disappointment could fill her he had her turned to face him. She wrapped her legs around his waist and her arms around his neck. He thrust back into her easily. God, she was so wet for him.

As he bit at the base of her neck she let him fuck her senseless. He started walking down the hallway with her pussy still encasing his dick. Curling her nails into his biceps, she bit her bottom lip. He instantly stopped moving inside of her. She groaned in frustration. In a few quick strides he was in his bedroom with the door slammed shut behind them. The room was too dark to really see anything, but she didn't need a visual. He had her in the center of the mattress only a second later, and was back inside of her, thrusting deep and long, and kissing the side of her neck again.

"I love the way you smell." He pumped into her slowly this time. "I love your flavor." He retreated and thrust back inside of her. He took her hands and lifted them above her head. He made love to her soft and slow, long and deep, and she felt another orgasm rising.

"Lucien," she breathed out.

"I love the way you feel, and I fucking love that you're all mine." He slammed into her, and the slow and long thrusting was gone. In its place was fast and hard, and so demanding and dominating.

"Fucking hell, Callie." His massive chest rose and fell from the force of his breathing. The sting of pain from his fingers digging into the sensitive flesh had her pleasure increasing. "I am going to tear you up." He spoke filthy, dirty, and it all turned her on. He certainly had showed her exactly what he was made of, but she wanted so much more. "You want that, don't you? You want me fucking you so damn hard you won't be able to sit for a week, so that you know who you belong to."

"God. *Lucien.*" The air left her. Did he actually expect her to answer? A tingling sensation traveled throughout her whole body at his sandpaper sounding voice. The corded muscle and tendons that were laced and bulging right underneath his flesh had the urge to lick and nip his skin consuming her.

The thick crest of his shaft pressed against the entrance of her pussy, and he held her gaze for a suspended moment before slamming into her with so much force she slid up the bed. A shocked cry left her when he bottomed out inside of her. Eyes wide and tears of agony and ecstasy slipping out of the corner of her eyes, she moaned for more.

"Look at me." Lucien's voice was deep and hard as he issued the command. When she did as he said everything around her faded until there was only this one moment in time. He hovered above her, his upper body blocking out the moonlight that spilled through the window. "I want you to watch while I slam my cock into your tight little pussy."

Callie lifted up and braced herself on her elbows. He slowly pulled out of her, and she watched as his length became visible inch after huge inch. His thickness was glossy from her wetness, and right when she thought he would torment her with just the tip lodged in her entrance, he thrust back into her. Arms shaking and breath leaving her in uneven gasps, Callie knew she couldn't hold out much longer. She needed to come … again.

****

Lucien watched his dick slide in and out of Callie's tight pussy. He wanted to go slow with her, make love to her and show her that she meant so much to him. But right now he was this fucking animal, needing her like a fiend. He didn't make love to her, no, he couldn't. He needed her like an addict, and it seemed she wanted him just as fiercely, too. Her flesh was pink and wet, swollen and gripped him like an iron-fist. Never had he wanted to be with a woman as badly as he did her, and it wasn't just about the sex, which was incredible. It was just being with *her*.

The slickness of her pussy and the suctioning warmth that surrounded him had his orgasm rushing precariously close to the surface. He pushed into her and pulled back out. Her luscious thighs had him imagining himself with his face buried between them, and her long dark hair had him picturing it fisted in his hand. Dipping his head to her hip he removed his hand and ran his tongue around her skin. Her moans were soft and breathy, and he worked his hips against hers. It was taking all of his strength to hold off the inevitable. He let his eyes travel up her rounded belly, the kind he absolutely loved, and to her large breasts. He had always been more of an ass-man, and boy, did she have one killer ass, but her tits were something of beauty. His pumping hips caused the globes to bounce up and down, and her nipples were tight, pink tips. His mouth watered for a taste, but at the moment he couldn't move as he became immobilized when she lifted her hips and met his thrusts.

He placed his hand back on her waist, and he dug his nails deeper into her smooth body. She arched her back when the head of his shaft scraped along her G-Spot. God, he could feel that engorged little bundle of tissue. He couldn't hold off from coming any longer. He needed this, needed to be with her in this way and fill her with his seed.

"Your cunt is all pink, wet, perfection, baby. Sucking at my dick like you're hungry for my cum." He was speaking so dirty to her, so raunchy that he should be ashamed. She as innocent in every way, and he was being a dirty fucking bastard.

His cock stretched her wide, and her inner muscles clenched around his girth. Arms and legs numb, he felt his orgasm move up his spine. She came for a third time, her pussy convulsing around his cock.

"That's it. Milk my fucking dick, Callie baby." Over and over he slid in and out of her, prolonging the intensity of their climaxes until she was thrashing her head on the bed. Her clit swelled with each down stroke he made, and when his thrusting increased even more she cried out. "Shit. I could fuck you all night long and never get enough." His sweat dripped onto her bouncing breasts, mixing with her own and sliding along her skin.

Once, twice, and on the third thrust he buried his erection so far in her that his balls slapped against her ass. He came and came even more, his body strained tight from the pleasure, and his cock twitching in her pussy as he emptied himself into her. "*God*, baby." His whole body shook, and although his orgasm was quite possibly the longest one in history, he never stopped slowly thrusting inside of her. With one final groan he stilled.

He pulled out of her, but when he went to get off the bed she pulled him toward her.

"Just hold me, Lucien. I don't care about the sweat or anything else. I just want you to hold me."

He smiled and moved back onto the bed, pulled her close to his body, and kissed her on the forehead. She lifted her hand and brushed away his sweaty hair. He craved her touch, craved her presence. She trusted him, and he fucking loved that. He reached between their bodies and ran his finger along her pussy hole. He felt their combined fluids seep out of her, but he pushed his finger back into her, not letting any of his cum leave her. Lucien wanted her filled with his seed, and that it was so far up inside of her that she'd be feeling the wetness of it come out of her tight little body for the next day.

She gasped, grabbed his wrist with a hand, but didn't pull his finger out of her. In fact, she pushed it in another inch. He growled out low, dipped his mouth toward her neck, and sucked at her flesh.

"I don't know what I did to earn a gift like you, Callie."

"Lucien—"

"No, baby, please let me say this." He kissed her again. "I've done a lot of fucked up shit in my life, hurt people, stolen and maimed, and just been an all around bastard, but when I look at you I feel like there is still good things in this world. What I feel for you borders on insane and possessive, but they are genuine emotions, *real* emotions, and I can swear to you that you will always be a priority to me."

She smiled, and he rested his forehead against hers.

"It has always been my club that was important to me. I have a family outside of the MC, obviously, but when it comes to loyalty, they have always had my back, always been there for me. But now I have you in my life, and I will never let you go."

"I'm not going anywhere, Lucien."

"I want you to have a life, a future, and going to school is a right step in that direction. I will always be here for you. I don't want you to ever worry about anything," he said softly.

She kissed him softly and rested her forehead on his chest. He held her head to him with a hand to the back of her head, and inhaled deeply. "You're mine, and I am yours. Forever. Irrevocably. Always." He stared in her eyes, making her see that he meant every damn word. "I meant it when I said you are mine, and there isn't anything on this planet that will ever take you away from me."

****

Cain sat on his Harley, took a hit off his smoke, and stared at the small house about an hour outside of River Run. He had spent a hell of a lot of time in prison, but he had finally rectified the situation, finished taking out the man that had hurt his daughter, and now he could move forward. There was movement behind the curtain, and his heart picked up pace. The one woman that had helped him through this entire process, never let up on giving him support, and had been the one to keep him updated on the motherfucker that he had just buried in the ground, was only a few feet away.

Violet Wings.

Her name was gentle, whimsical even, but the woman that he had know for longer than he could even remember, wasn't just the person who had given him the location of the asshole he had wasted, but the one woman that he shouldn't want because of who she was.

You shouldn't be here, just watching her like a fucking stalker, waiting to get a glimpse of her.

He took one more inhale from his cigarette and snubbed it out on the heel of his boot before flicking it aside. Yeah, he should leave, but he couldn't. Serving nine out of the sixteen years he was sentenced hadn't taught him anything aside from exacting his vengeance when he got out. His brothers had been there for him the entire time, as was his daughter. But it was Violet that had kept writing him despite the fact he told her to forget about him, to move on with her life, and put all of this shit behind her. She wasn't just the woman that his daughter had been best friends with while growing up, she was also a victim of that sadistic bastard he had had the pleasure of killing.

He had never told anyone that Violet had been hurt by that asshole. He hadn't told his club, and not even his daughter. Violet had told him in confidence, kept that shit inside of her for years after the fact, and he had taken pleasure in ending that bastard's life for his little girl and the woman that he had grown to care about more than he should.

Getting off of his bike, walking toward her front door, and knowing he shouldn't be doing this couldn't have stopped him. He had only seen her once, years after they had started talking on the phone and in letters, and that was when she had come to the prison. That had been the only time because he had told her not to come back, that the shithole he was living in for all those years was not a place he wanted her to be at. And she had listened, thank fuck, because the men that lived in the prison were not good. Cain wasn't good, never was, and would resort to things to make his point known, or to protect what was his. He was dangerous, violent, and that was just who he was, who he would always be.

He found himself standing in front of her door, his hand curled into a fist to knock on the scarred wood, but before he could do that the front door opened and there she stood. Her dark hair was in a braid over her shoulder, and her bright green eyes were wide as she watched him with a mixture of emotion.

Fuck, this was wrong for him to be here.

"I wondered if you were going to come to me when you got out," she said softly.

He cleared his throat, not sure what to say.

"I stayed away, knowing that was what you wanted." She glanced down, and when she lifted just her gaze to his, Cain's fucking heart stopped in his chest.

"I wasn't going to come here, was going to stay away because your life is better off without me in it." He scrubbed a hand over his jaw. The last few months had been a whirlwind of him taking care of business, and deciding what he was going to do next.

"I'm glad you came, Cain." She smiled softly, looking down again. When she stepped aside, letting him in, he cursed himself for taking that first step forward. That was the beginning of the end, because what Violet didn't know, shit, what no one knew, was that he fucking cared about her. He *loved* her, had loved her for years even though he was a bastard and didn't deserve to feel such an emotion. She was his daughter's best friend, had been raped by the man that had tried to do the same thing to his baby girl, and was twenty years younger than he was. He was going to ruin her life with his toxicity. But fuck, he couldn't stop himself or his feelings, and only saw them getting more intense now that she was here with him in the flesh, and they didn't have plastic or phones separating them.

Epilogue

One Year Later

The house was insane with all the activity, and it was only going to get even more hectic as everyone continued to come over. Callie had come home for Thanksgiving, and she was currently holding her baby brother. Marcus was only a few months old, and he already had bright blue eyes like she shared with her father, and a thatch of black hair. He slept, the bottle Callie currently held in his mouth now empty. She pulled it away, wiped his little lips, and lifted him over her shoulder to gently pat his back.

The guys from the club were already at Kink and Cookie's house. The noise was pretty loud, but Marcus was sleeping through it all. Cookie poked her head around the corner, her nose dotted with flour from the pie she was baking, and her smile wide.

"You holding up?"

"You kidding? I'm a champ at this. It almost makes me want to have one of my own," Callie teased softly and smiled.

"Don't get any ideas of having any of those until you're done with college," her dad said and smiled. He kissed Cookie on the lips, and she disappeared back into the kitchen. Kink walked into the living room and looked down at Marcus. "He sure is something, isn't he?"

Marcus started fussing lightly, and she handed her baby brother to her father.

"He really is." She stood and ran her fingers along the little tuft of dark hair on his head.

"I remember when you were this little. You cried so much when your mother held you." He smiled at the memory. "Made me feel proud as hell when you'd stop fussing when you were in my arms."

She laughed softly.

"But you're not a baby anymore. All grown up, working toward your business degree, and living your life." Kink stared at her. "You make me so damn proud, sweetheart." The sound of a vehicle pulling up told her Lucien had finally arrived. Kink leaned down and kissed her on the top of the head. "Go on. I know it's been a couple of weeks since you saw him, and he's been bitching up a storm on missing you."

She felt her cheeks heat at her dad's words.

"I swear he is one cranky bastard when you're not around," her father said that with a hard tone in his voice, but then he smiled. He turned and left her alone, and she went to the window.

Lucien climbed out of his SUV, saw her right away, and gave her a wink. God, she heated instantly at that small gesture. She met him at the door, and as soon as he was right in front of her he had her in his arms. She was off her feet, and then he moved them inside to the foyer, closed the door behind him, and kissed her senseless. He tasted good, minty and sweet, and her body remembered everything about him in startling clarity.

"I missed you, baby."

"I missed you, too," she responded, and held on tighter to his thick biceps. For the last year she had focused on school, coming home during the weekends, and spending as much time with Lucien as possible. It was hard being away from him, but she had to do this for herself, had to make something out of her life so she could be with him and have had an accomplishment under her belt. Getting her business degree sounded like the right step to take, because Lucien and the club were her life, and she wanted to be near him when she was finished with school. She could help manage the books, keep the paperwork in line, and still be near her family and the man she loved. But for the last two weekends she had stayed on campus, studying for her semester finals. It felt like forever since she had seen him, but then times like these made it all worthwhile.

Lucien pulled back, gently lowered her to the ground, and looked at her in the eyes. "I don't want to disrespect your dad in his own house, but we will definitely be finishing this later on." He kissed her softly on the lips and set her on her feet. Kink may huff and gruff at times, but he had accepted their relationship. All of the members had. They were one giant family, loyal to the end, and having so much love for each other that there was never a shortage of it.

"I love you, Callie," Lucien said against her mouth, and she felt him smile.

"And I love you." And she did, so much so that at times it was almost painful, but it was a discomfort she wanted, yearned for, and hoped never ended. This was her life, and the road she had taken to get here had been bumpy, but she wouldn't have changed it for anything.

The End

www.jenikasnow.com

JENIKA SNOW

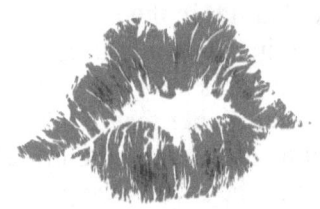

EVERNIGHT PUBLISHING ®

www.evernightpublishing.com